THE LIZARDS

THE

LIZARDS

Alessandra Lavagnino

Translated from the Italian by William Weaver

HARPER & ROW, PUBLISHERS
New York, Evanston, San Francisco, London

For Mario

"Ma come gli occhi a quel bel volto mise
Gli ne venne pietade, e non l'uccise."
—L. ARIOSTO, *Orlando Furioso*, xix, 10

THE LIZARDS

I WAS STANDING under the big picture—a seascape with two boats and water that looked like real water—and it never crossed my mind to sit down. I was glad I had to wait, and I actually didn't mind being alone so much.

"I've just phoned him; you can go," my mother had said.

"I'll take you, baby," Elide had said then.

"No, you have to go somewhere else for me. Besides, why does anybody have to go with her? Don't start giving her ideas. And her name isn't Baby."

I had been in that waiting room other times, but with my mother and on her account. I knew everything I would find in the next room; I knew the click the door would make when it opened, and I was expecting it.

"Mamma's not with you? All by yourself, eh?" the dentist asked. He opened the door wider, leaned forward to look around; then he motioned me inside and shut the door again.

"Ye-yes," I said, with an effort. I needn't have answered, I thought, a moment later. I began to swallow several times, in spite of myself, one lump after another in my throat. I climbed into the chair.

"Now let's see," the dentist said. "Open wide." His

hands smelled freshly of disinfectant soap; the little mirror and the instrument he put in my mouth were wet, cold; they came from a glass filled with a white liquid and other instruments. I held my breath while the steel tip investigated the cavity in my premolar. It hurt, and I didn't move.

I looked at the hairs of his blondish eyebrows, the hairs in his nose. He turned, and picked up a wisp of cotton with his pincers, wetted it with liquid from a phial and filled the hole in my tooth. The pink paste he used to close the cavity smelled of carnations.

"Let's see the rest now." With his little mirror he looked everywhere; he took a little rod from his glass and tapped my teeth. A canine hurt, and I jumped.

"Next Thursday at the same time. Tell Mamma."

I went down the steps, the carnation flavor of the pink paste in my mouth, so fast that the steps slipped beneath my feet. I had said good-bye without noticing; or maybe I hadn't said it.

When I went through the door of our building, I realized I didn't want to go up right away. So I went to the concierge. I found her sewing, her swollen feet on a chair.

"Marzietta, what are you up to? Where are you coming from?" she asked, without turning around.

"From there," I said. I didn't want to say anything else.

"There? Where's that?"

"Across the street."

"And who's over there? The dentist?"

"Ye-yes."

"You went by yourself, did you? You had to take him something?"

I didn't answer. She would believe I'd nodded a yes with my head; that's what I thought. She didn't ask me anything else.

2

Then I went home. Elide wasn't back yet, and I began to play with the cat. I breathed my carnation perfume into his face while we were together under the dining-room table.

The door of the study was closed, but through the milky glass I could see the light over the great desk, and I could almost smell the cigarette smoke that by now would have filled the room. I could hear my mother's voice, a man's voice, another woman's whining voice. Four women were in the waiting room. A bad afternoon for my mother.

When Elide came in, she thought I hadn't come back yet, so she headed straight for the kitchen without looking for me. Then, as she went by, she saw me.

"Baby, you're down there. Did it hurt? Tell me. Were you afraid? Come to Elide. Come to your old Elide."

Reluctantly, I came from under the table, annoyed by her delay.

"I was just about to go and collect you, I really was. Tell me: Did it hurt?"

"No."

I didn't want to talk about it. Couldn't she understand?

I WENT BY Via Marianna Dionigi and I saw that they had torn down the building. The street is unrecognizable with that gap.

As for the apartment, I knew I could only remember it—Giulia, the concierge, is dead, too—but I thought I would find the street again, the same, with its rich secrets. A gloomy street, shy of its own bright view toward the Tiber; pretentious buildings and incongruous food stores, redolent of cheese, anchovies, salami. No other street has such appetizing odors beneath houses where you imagine no one eats. We ate very little and I can't forget the feeling of extreme bareness and cold I had when I passed with Elide beneath the hanging chickens, their necks stretched out of proportion, their eyes shut, the lids' edges like little coronets. And it is a street that retains its smells: the sweet aroma of chocolate that enshrouded the Unica shop on the corner seems to remáin there, around the walls, even now when the Unica has moved away and Adamoli Variety Store has moved in.

So the house is no more: spaces, walls, surfaces known to my touch; switches I could still find in the dark; matter that exists no more is matter no longer: memory now.

I REMEMBER NOTHING of the house in Via Flaminia where I was born except an immense impression of white light, as if from a skylight, and long shelves along the wall with cages and cages of shrieking little birds. Suddenly the birds come close, and I can see my father's neck, cheek, ear, hair; I am on his shoulder. But Elide said it wasn't true, we had no bird cages in Via Flaminia, and we didn't live under a skylight, so it must be some other memory; but Elide never helped me rediscover the true one. "No, it was Elena who kept canaries, but when were you ever at Elena's? Yes, I did take you there once, but you were still a tiny baby, you can't remember."

Of Via Marianna Dionigi I remember the cobblestones very close to my eyes and the two huge stone workers in white undershirts who, in turn, let a heavy wooden club fall on the cobbles, driving them into the soft sand that swells and pours from the crevices. My little hand is in Elide's hand, rough, smelling always of bleach.

4

We went only to buy eggs at the shops where the chickens were hung up. We never ate chicken because my mother didn't like it, but sometimes I had it at my grandmother's, in Via Pietro Cavallini, which is a street without shops and such shops as it has are there by mistake: a silent, bright street, where the half-moon pattern of the cobblestones seems wider.

I went to my grandmother's only with Elide, who always had mysterious things to tell her; they would slip into the little room beyond the kitchen, under the chandelier made of a curtain of little glass tubes which tinkled when they were struck; there the sewing machine stayed and the big wardrobe: I asked how it had got through the door. "It was little when it came in, and then it grew up," my grandmother said; and it must have been true, I thought, because the enormous piece of furniture had a very tiny key and keyhole. The smell of "clothes to sew" which that wardrobe contained was different from the smell of sewn clothes in all the wardrobes I came to know afterward. Maria the dressmaker worked in that room and I thought she had got her wrinkled lip from the pins she held in her mouth when she was trying a dress on me or on Grandmother. I knew no worse torture than having to stand still while Maria the dressmaker set in the sleeves, pinning them and singing, in her Sicilian dialect: "You have to suffer if you want to be beautiful."

In those years Grandmother and Maria the dressmaker made my clothes, except for the ready-made ones my mother bought. My shoes too could be distinguished as those from Grandmother and those bought by my mother. In Grandmother's house the word "buy" didn't exist; you said "pick." "Your mother picked this for you, ready-made," they would say, and Maria the dressmaker would raise her eyes and purse her wrinkled lips, shaking her gray head slightly. I felt a sad bewilderment that tarnished the joy and pride in my new dress bought in the big brightly lighted department store.

My grandmother was very small and seemed bodiless; I was surprised to see Maria the dressmaker make new clothes for her, because to me it seemed she always had on the same dress and it never wore out. I remember her face and her hands less well than that dress of hers and her shoes. She wore low black shoes, a bit pointed, with a strap and button, and a little heel. Shoes very like the ones she bought for me, also with strap and button. Her shoes were divided into old and new, and she changed them several times a day. I never managed to wear out my black ones with the strap because I wore them only "to go somewhere," whereas for school and "for everyday" I had brown ones with laces, like a boy's, which my mother bought. I can see my feet, wearing one pair or the other, going from slab to slab of the sidewalk, skipping over the cracks.

From the window of Grandmother's kitchen, suspended in the midst of the courtyard's rectangular sky, I saw the Zeppelin one afternoon.

I went with Elide to the little gardens in Piazza Cavour. At the end of the sidewalk of Via Marianna Dionigi, she would let go of my hand, grasp my wrist much harder, and we crossed the street. She wouldn't let me step on the tram tracks for fear of a shock. On the opposite sidewalk she took my hand and drew me rapidly past the sharp ammonia smell that came from the urinal, saying, "Hold your breath." Elide established many prohibitions for me: Don't look, don't go there; don't move; don't sweat; don't drink now that you're overheated; don't think about it; don't take off your coat; and we'll bring a little jacket along because later it'll turn cool. I hated the little jackets that Elide put on me later when it turned cool. I hated the bathrobe of pink flannel, immortal

6

garment, obligatory in the morning and evening hours of certain pinched holidays of ours at Marino. The house there had a little privy at one end of a big terrace, and at evening, before going to bed, when I had to cross the terrace, I shielded my eyes with my hand, to keep from seeing the stars that filled me with abysmal terror.

I never played with the other children in Piazza Cavour, because they were older and Elide was afraid they would shove me, knock me down and give me whooping cough. I don't remember having any friends before I went to school. But there was a little boy, son of some friends of my mother's, who used to come to the house. His name was Titti, and he was very beautiful, with black curls all over his head. He terrorized me. He was strong and full of energy; he broke my toys and ran into me with his scooter. Once, throwing my ball, he broke a blue glass vase and tried to make me say I had done it. "You're her little girl and she won't do anything to you," he said. This instigation to lie and this idea made a deep impression on me; I thought about those words for a long time.

Elide talked uninterruptedly in rapid little whispers when she was alone. Even in the street. I wondered who her imaginary listener might be and if it was always the same one; and I thought it was just one, since she spoke to him so much.

In summer I went with my mother to Ostia. Elide prepared our bathing suits, a little bottle of milk, two sandwiches, and put everything in a bamboo hamper you could close by sliding a bamboo rod as long as the hamper itself through four eyelets. Our cat had traveled in that hamper. My mother wore low shoes of canvas and rubber, and, striding along, she dragged me after her to the tram, the Circolare Nera. At Ponte Garibaldi we changed to the Circolare Rossa, which for me was already the tram to Ostia, since I never took it for any other place. At the Pyramid we got off and it was already late, my mother dragged me on, and a stone got into my shoe, but I kept quiet while we were at the ticket window, and then on the platform with little squares like chocolate bars, and on the train so low you could enter it with one step.

Now all the ladies carry straw baskets, but a cat wouldn't fit into all of them, as I calculate, looking at them carefully. All the children swing their tanned legs from the seats; their feet, bare, in sandals, don't touch the floor. I don't dare swing my legs, because I'm a little girl without any brothers and I am with my mother, who is reading a book. A bee comes through the window and walks on the glass; from below it starts up two, four times, falling back, and my mother doesn't drive it away. But soon you can smell the sea, which is the smell of the train, too, the warm wood of the cabins, the crunch of sand beneath sandals and the feet of the beach boy whose big toe is horribly far from his other toes. I'm afraid of the sea smell. My mother undresses me in the stuffy heat of the cabin; we run barefoot on the catwalks, slabs of hard cement; we run on the burning sand and then my mother picks me up and carries me, still running, into the water, holding me high up, and, when the water reaches her chest, suddenly she submerges me, because that's how to do it, it's good for you like that; and the sea enters my ears like a thousand little pieces of glass, hitting one another, in my eyes, all burning and whirling light, until she pulls me up again and clasps me to her, laughing, but I'm still afraid.

Then, on the sand, bundled up in a Turkish towel, I drink the milk Elide gave me and I drink it from the bottle, my eyes closed against the sunny sky, a little gurgle in my throat.

8

"The black shark! The black shark!" Peppino says, coming up, dripping from the sea. He has a black suit with shoulder straps and he is all red in the face, laughing. I laugh too.

"The black shark!" Then he and I make a deep hole near the water, while my mother sits farther back with her friends. The women have thick braids around their heads, big eyes, and they speak in slow, deep voices, full of echoes, letting the warm black sand trickle through their long fingers in an absent-minded game. They are friends she meets only at Ostia. In Rome she has no women friends, only men, colleagues, and all the people who come to the house ask for the lawyer. "Is the lawyer in?" they say. She's the lawyer. My father used to call her that, too, but smiling, joking. "So long, lawyer," he would say, and she gave him her hand, in the hall. The two of them, hand in hand! I remember them coming along a meadow, I don't know where, in the sunlight. I remember him, very tall, picking me up and swinging me around near the ceiling, as if in another world. He died when I was still little. Many people were in the house, and they told me he had gone away and then that he was dead. I never saw my mother again as she had been in those years when he was there. And for a while, it seems to me, she also disappeared from my days.

At home Mother stood up to dress the salad, and in the twisted horn spoon she dissolved salt in the vinegar, pursing her lips.

I had measles and Elide read *The Blue Bird* to me, but she read slowly and badly. Then she went to the kitchen, leaving me alone with the book. My mother came in and said, "Give it to me." She was dressed to go out; she sat on the edge of the chair. She began again at the beginning, but very fast, so the book lasted only a brief, embarrassed time.

"There," she said at the end. "You like the Dark Prince, eh? You like him?" And as she showed me the illustration of the Dark Prince I was ashamed of him and of my whole book.

WHEN I WAS ALONE in the house, I went to the big mirror in my mother's bedroom. I looked first at my hair and forehead; then at my mouth, which I started moving; then my eyes. I made faces at myself and I plunged into fear at that horrible sight. Then I was engulfed in terror that the frightful thing in the mirror somehow belonged to me, in some way was me. It was impossible, it couldn't be true. That thing facing me wasn't me, had nothing to do with me. And yet it must. So, with terror, I realized that it was I who didn't belong to that image which nevertheless existed; in fact—and this became clear, true, the only true thing—I wasn't there, I didn't exist because there was nothing around —around, down, down, as if in a well whose walls contract as you try in vain to grasp them—there was nothing around me—less and less all the time, less than less—that I could hold on to, nothing that gave a reason, a reality to my existence.

Afterward it was no longer necessary for me to make faces at myself: I had only to look in the mirror. And then the memory of that experience was enough. At some moment, it might seize me, anywhere, at any moment, without warning. I had no connection with the rest. But this didn't mean the rest lost reality: I was the one who was no longer there.

It was horrible. And yet the memory—the possibility— of my dangerous and forbidden game became a haven, a con-

10

solation, something apart, a reserve. This lasted for several years, in spurts. Then, I almost forgot it.

AS SOON AS I WOKE UP I saw a little silverfish that ran along the wall and hid behind the picture. There the wall-paper must have kept its old, darker color, and little slivers of light filtered in where the frame didn't touch: an enormous space for the silverfish, who could eat a bit of paint there, a bit of sugary paste, perhaps the remains of a spider and his web. In this way, I was as tiny as the silverfish.

"Marzia, time to get up. You'll be late for school."

My mother, with her morning voice, guttural and harsh. During the day then, she spoke so much, with her clients and in court, that her voice softened. But not for me: in the evening she was too tired to talk. She went to bed right after supper and read a whole thriller to the last page; falling asleep, she dropped the book to the floor. There it remained till morning, when Elide picked it up and put it in the row with the others. When she had filled the shelf she would collect them all, talking to herself, tie up two packets with string and go sell them. The money she received was hers.

I went to school in fear. It was a light, stubborn apprehension that clenched my stomach at breakfast, making it small and high, it seemed to me.

"Eat, Marzia."

"My stomach's little."

"Nonsense."

My fear was of not being able to answer the questions at school.

11

"Eat, Marzia."

I swallowed; then: "My stom . . . achslit . . . tle. . . ."

"Nonsense."

The schoolmistress was good, but she asked me what a tributary was.

"Tell me what a tributary is."

"A . . . a . . ."

"A tributary. Go ahead."

"It's . . . a . . . a river that . . . that flows into . . ."

I used easier words instead of the ones that I would have liked to say, so my answers were hardly my own; often, as I knew, they were incorrect.

I don't know how much the other girls looked at me because I always kept my eyes on my shoes, against the worn edge of the platform. When I reached my seat, Claudia greeted me the first time with "What happened to you? What's wrong?" Then no more. Then she watched me come back, red and sweating, in silence, and after a while she would say something else.

Claudia had red hair and freckles; they said she was rich and that's why she lived with her mother in a hotel.

THE TENTH OF JUNE was Claudia's birthday and I had been invited to the party in her hotel at Trinità dei Monti. The invitation had been issued to me long before, perhaps months ahead, since I remember the waiting and my long anxiety that I wouldn't be able to peel an orange with my knife and fork. I was very much concerned with this business of the orange which I was reminded of at the table day after day,

12

and it seemed there was no one I could ask for advice: my mother peeled her orange with a single, long, helicoid turn of the knife, in silence.

Claudia's party was as unreal as I had imagined it. Claudia's red curls were tighter than usual, and she received her friends in the garden. But she took me—"Just for a minute, come, come with me a minute"—up to her room, after stairways and corridors covered with carpets, and there was her mother, slender and silent, who smiled a lot at me. Claudia opened a closet with a sliding door—I had never seen anything like it—and showed me the new dress her mamma had given her, and it was a dress that resembled her very much, I think, green, light and transparent as it was. Her mother smiled at us in silence, embarrassed. I had never thought a mamma could seem so shy.

No oranges to peel. At the party there were sweets and ices the like of which nobody had ever seen and lots of boys of whom I was jealous, all at little tables in a garden which may have been a terrace made of little flower beds and paths and fountains.

"Come, sit here," a dark governess said to me, as she was feeding some Japanese twins two years old. I sat opposite her and ate cake and ices as the governess went on filling the children, telling me she had come from Spain with the twins and their mamma because in Spain there was a revolution which was "very dangerous" and she herself was Spanish.

I listened to her; and in later years, when the war came, I often said to myself, I wonder where those Japanese twins are with their mamma and the Spanish governess. I imagined them far away, in strange places, because it seemed right and certain to me that the little wandering group should continue to enjoy immunity from wars and have for themselves, always, gardens like the one in Claudia's hotel, and sweets and colored ices.

THE FEW TIMES I went out with my mother I gave her my hand, as I did with Elide.

"Go on, walk by yourself. At your age! You're not my puppy; you're a big girl! Go on!"

When my hands were free, I didn't know what to do with them; I stuffed them into my pockets.

"Go on, I'm going to have those pockets of yours sewn up. What a tiresome habit." And she really did have them sewn up, or else she bought me dresses without pockets.

"When are you ever going to grow? Are you really going to have such tiny feet? Woman's feet. Feet for high heels."

Sudden, searing, the longing for my father gripped me, and the sweet memory of him became more and more a dream. My mother never spoke to me about him.

IN THE GINNASIO, there was a little girl in my class, with bent shoulders and very skinny legs, a little pointed face with thick down on her lip and hollow eyes, very black and grim. Her name was Giorgina Riva and I don't know what sicknesses or handicaps she had had in the past, or if this past was known to our teachers. She spoke in a low voice, she moved slowly and the physical education instructor showed

14

special regard for her. She was diligent and neat, always present, but not clever. When she was called to be questioned, she would stand very close to the teacher's desk and speak without interruptions, in her soft way, moving her head back and forth like a pigeon. The teacher would lean toward her, listening and looking at a corner of the desk. I believe she had no fear of teachers.

We didn't sit next to each other, and for years a mute, awkward friendship developed between us, unknown to all the others, a friendship made up of smiles. But what I felt for her was, basically, an unpleasant sensation; admiration diseased with dark envy.

"SLOWLY. Speak slowly. More slowly. Take it easy!" my mother would say, with a slowing gesture of her hand, but without patience. "Think of the words before you say them. Think of them one at a time."

But I did think of them one at a time, those words. I thought of them: and the words—one by one—loomed up in front of me like cliffs, and after the spasm in my mouth and four gulps of saliva, I would stop, blocked. Then I would start again more slowly and I would choose other words; I tried to take them by surprise, from the side, these words, catch them and say them before they too could turn into cliffs. The worst were the words that I knew had stopped me other times.

"Have you studied your history?" my mother said, since I liked that subject very much. "Do you know it?"

"Ye-yes, I've lear—" I gulped—"learned it."

"Where are you?"

15

"The . . . the . . . fall . . . of the . . ." I gulped, gulped again. "Roman . . ."

"Good. You know it then?"

". . . Empire." How silly, I thought, I could have stopped with "Romans." I had to learn, learn to economize.

And, very slowly, I really learned to save many words. But it always seemed I hadn't learned enough, and I was determined to become more clever and sly, to evade and trick that enemy who was both inside me and outside me, but who, I thought proudly, was more outside me than inside.

IN THAT PERIOD my mother gave me money. "Do what you want with it," she said. I didn't know what to do with it and I kept the two lire or the five lire a week.

"What? You still have all of it? Well, I'll give you the same again. And by the end of the week you must have spent it. Learn the value of money."

I learned to spend that money or to give it away, in alms hardly charitable, shoving the coins into the poor boxes in churches. I didn't feel it was mine; at first something indifferent, the money, when I was ordered to spend it, became a burden. No relationship was established between that money and me, and I continued to stand spellbound outside shopwindows where even cheap things still seemed unattainable, because I wasn't sure of my taste and I would never have dared come home with an item of clothing, an object whose choice might have been criticized. I was also afraid to go in. I constructed a long sentence to say to the shopkeeper; then, knowing that I would be blocked at the first word, I stayed outside.

I bought old books on the bookstalls by the bridge, or behind Zingone's department store, at the Maddalena. After I had picked up a number of them, I would hold one out to the bookseller, pay him and go on my way content.

"What are you reading? For heaven's sake! Find something more amusing, more modern, something that'll teach you what life's about nowadays. You don't have a scrap of curiosity. At your age, don't you feel like reading forbidden books? Don't you children lend each other books that are a bit dirty? Oh, the younger generation!"

Those references in the plural, that "generation," were a way of consoling herself for the fact that it wasn't "they" who were like that, but only me, her daughter.

And I bought wool. Wool to knit sweaters that I got all wrong and then didn't like. "What a color!" she said. "All huddled over those needles, you make me feel cold just to look at you. You work and work, and what do you do? I never see anything finished."

I thought I should knit a pullover for her, and maybe she would be pleased, but the certainty that I wouldn't pick the right color, that I would make mistakes, made me give it up. Besides, I couldn't bear the idea of having to try the pullover on her.

With the money—her money, as I always thought of it—I bought some presents for her, but she forgot about them and I was offended. I was very nasty and quick to take offense.

My grandmother said to me, "Tell your mother Giulia Giorgi died."

For many days, as soon as I was with my mother, I was assailed by the thought, Now I must tell her, now I'll tell her, and it paralyzed me: because I was terrified of doing and saying unpleasant things, repulsed by other people's

17

emotions, or by other people observing my emotions.

"Marzia, did you tell your mamma Giulia Giorgi died? She used to be very fond of her."

"N-no . . . I for . . . I forgot."

"Tell her today. And ask her if she has my emerald brooch. I think she has it. That's for you, remember. When you grow up, you can wear it."

More days went by, and in the evening I looked at the picture over my bed and I couldn't sleep. I rehearsed, I repeated the words I had chosen, the most indirect ones possible: "Mamma, has Elide told you about the death of Giulia Giorgi?" Above all, I wasn't to block after "the death," I kept telling myself; and I could already see her eyes widen, waiting.

And when I finally managed to tell my mother this thing—in the street, looking at the ground, and I did block after "the death"—my mother had already heard the news. I didn't know who that Giulia Giorgi was.

"What about the brooch? Did you ask her about the brooch? It's yours, remember."

Then the brooch, which had seemed something negligible compared to the death of Giulia Giorgi, became enormous over the years, a monstrous silence with me. I never asked my mother about it; and this omission reproached me, crushingly, along with all my other guilt which came later: precisely because my grandmother never mentioned it to me again.

"YOU DON'T KNOW ANYTHING. You aren't interested in anything. Are all you young people like that? You all live like snails. Do you know the war is about to break out? Do you know that?"

18

I knew it and I was dying of fear, but I didn't speak.

We went to Santa Severa for the summer of 1939, and then the summer of 1940, and I lost my appetite and couldn't sleep. But the days went by and I saw that after all the sun hadn't turned dark and the grownups went on living as before. In the morning they went to the beach, and with an effort of their arms and hairy legs they put up gaily colored umbrellas, and in the afternoon, wearing huge sunglasses, they went to eat ices, and in the evening they went dancing.

The winters in Rome were calm. Food was rationed, and perhaps the smells of Via Marianna Dionigi had faded a little and changed. We had the blackout, but it changed very little in my life.

The last summer at Santa Severa was in 1942; we were just Grandmother, Elide and me. The other little villas were empty. Only—and she lived there all year round—there was the mistress of the elementary school.

Beyond a vast, uncultivated field, from our house you could see the Children's Summer Colony, a big L-shaped building, which didn't house any children that summer but airmen instead. We heard their voices, their shouts, some shooting at times. We saw them jump down from a springboard, practicing how to land with a parachute.

We were already hungry, even if the worst was yet to come. "A touch of hunger," Elide would say, and often in the morning, instead of going to the beach, we went to glean among the fields between the Via Aurelia and the railroad line. Then we ate that wheat boiled. The earth was dry, red, hot; the stubble hurt my feet in my sandals of cloth and imitation leather. There were cicadas on the ilexes along the road and locusts everywhere, the kind with blue or red wings which I could also see on the beach, flying over the little dunes with flowering thistles.

We didn't talk. We sat on the ground to gather the

grain that lay around there, and I would stare spellbound at a big black ant, without any dust, who was dragging away, by himself, a whole ear of wheat. My thin legs were tanned and peeling, and I wore a cotton dress with blue and white checks that Grandmother had made for me by herself: Maria the dressmaker no longer came to her.

In the afternoon we went to pick chicory, and sometimes Grandmother came along. She would sit on a low wall—her feet in the black shoes with straps didn't touch the ground—and she would tell us old stories she knew by heart, about when she was a little girl and lived at Ascoli and Grandmother Caterina—her grandmother—sent her to school in a litter across the snow: she was so tiny and light they were afraid she would catch cold. Elide and I had short, sharp knives and we cut the chicory plants a bit below the leaves which were flat against the ground, just at the little stem before the white, bitter root.

Then we would go out on the Via Aurelia, its asphalt still hot from the sun, and walk to Cantinone, the big farm where there was an "authorized" store, and it would devour our coupons, giving us in exchange a little bread, some cheese and no canned goods. The floor was of old planks, which resounded hollowly, impregnated with wine and trampled spit.

From Cantinone, along the fenced-off, white road, we went to the Castello. I liked the Castello because it was a village, with shady streets, where the furrows of hardened mud and of fertilizer lasted, and there were chickens. The milk woman lived at the Castello, and she always had to be sent for: tall and red, she had a face covered with freckles and always talked about her son, a fat boy as red as she was, while she gave us the milk, carefully measured out from a big aluminum container. As we went home along the beach we passed the Colony and, seen from nearby, that banal building came alive with details, its stucco all stained; the soldiers were no longer the gesticulating marionettes they seemed from our house, but men with faces and hands.

At sunset the beach looked burnt; the shingle was broader and, it seemed to me, softer than in the morning. I took off my sandals, turned up my skirt and ran, splashing, in the warm water. At low tide, I lingered sometimes with Elide, digging for cockles, plunging my arm into the water and searching with my fingers in the soft sand, ribbed like little waves; then we took the cockles home and put them in a bucket, but I don't remember ever eating them.

At night, I thought again of their life, in their shells, stuck in the sand of the seabed with the heavy, shifting water over them, in the dark. Do cockles have eyes? And is day different from night for them? And why, when they have a choice between lying inert or crawling over the sand, do they sometimes decide to crawl and sometimes lie still? I asked myself these idle questions in the darkness of the night swollen by the chirping of the crickets.

I don't know how many days we had been at Santa Severa, in that wartime summer that was motionless for us, when the soldier began coming to see us. He wasn't tall, and he was awkward in that blue-gray uniform, too big for him, but soon his figure on the little road and then at our gate became a friendly, awaited sight. Elide had brought him to us—a boy far from his home, she said—but it was with my grandmother then that he conversed, sitting on the porch. She asked him specific questions about his life as a peasant in Calabria, and he answered in short sentences that followed one another, numerous, so that his speech had the unexpected, steady flow of a little stream. I was silent—a summer without words, that one—but I let myself follow the pleasant stream of that talk whose unfamiliar dialect didn't seem ugly to me. And I thought of the mosquitoes that were surely finding at that moment some crevices through which to enter the house.

One day the soldier told us they gave him too much bread, far more than he could eat, and he brought us two round loaves. After that, he brought us two of those small loaves every day. My grandmother said we didn't need them, he shouldn't deprive himself; Elide thanked him and took the loaves into the house. It was very good bread.

We took walks with him, Elide and I. One morning we were at the mouth of a canal, where the water, meeting the sea, turned yellow and foaming, when we saw an airplane close to the sea, giving off a frightful stream of smoke, blacker and blacker. It came down, crashed, slid along the water and sank, the black smoke suddenly extinguished in the sunlight. We hadn't heard a sound.

None of us said a word, but I saw that the soldier, instead of looking at that point on the sea, was looking at me with an expression of concern and sorrow. The sky was full of sun, and metal objects glistened for a little while on the smooth, blue water. The soldier insisted on taking us home at once.

I was coming back with Elide from the Castello one afternoon, and there was low tide. The soldiers were bathing in front of the Colony. We didn't see our soldier right away and I was the one who called to him when I glimpsed him; he joined us, with embarrassment, and we went away together from his stretch of sea, entering ours. He started hunting cockles with us. He found a large number, and he was happy and laughing while we stood in the warm water up to our knees, and the sun was setting on the red, flat sea.

The next day, when we came back from our walk, we found the soldier at the house, sitting on a step of the porch, with his shoes in the zinnia bed, while Grandmother crocheted in her usual chair. They were silent and a dark apprehension seized me at that immobile scene in the light of dusk which has no distances. But the two moved, seeing us arrive, and I forgot the immobile sense of eternity that had struck me a moment before. We spent what little remained of the evening outside, as the mosquitoes entered the house.

As he left, the soldier told us that perhaps the next day they would be shipping him out, and he asked us, if we cared to give it to him, for our address in Rome. My grandmother gave him the address of Via Pietro Cavallini. Again I felt my heart gripped and I realized what the anguish I had felt earlier had been; but I didn't know I had grown fond of the soldier, and perhaps the whole summer had been without depth, like that light after the sunset.

At the end of September there was no more stubble, and the beach had turned dark brown, hard, pocked by drops of rain. The wheels of the rare bicycles made a faint, crackling sound in the wet dust of the road to the Castello and left trails that crossed and recrossed, winding into infinity.

We went back to Rome, to our streets. A letter came to Via Pietro Cavallini: a letter from the soldier, as we realized. It was for me—for Miss Marzia—and the writer asked me to answer, because he was on a desert island, alone, and a thousand fierce animals surrounded him and they were sure to devour him if Miss Marzia, who was the only one who could, didn't deliver him from such a horrible end.

"Why, this is a love letter!" my grandmother said, as Elide laughed into her clasped hands and I looked at my shoes.

say, when the groans started. I went and tried to calm her, and I felt grown-up, the mistress of another human being. The intoxicating sensation of possession lasted; I stayed even when Elide dozed off and her eyes, which were never entirely closed, grew dull.

My mother went in there early in the morning, as she had that first time, for a few minutes. In silence, at the door, she sipped her coffee, staring at the immense face, soft and white; then she went off again until the next day.

In the morning I was the one who picked up the thriller beside my mother's bed and took it into Elide's room. There the books piled up and I started reading them for hours and hours.

"Marzia, Marzia, where are you?" my mother called, and in silence I sprang into the hall and, only then, answered, out of breath, "I'm coming."

Carlotta Moi tended that body in silence and went to empty the contents of the pot in our bathroom, never in her own. We bought cloths and absorbent pads which were never changed often enough. Elide complained then, and I went to say so, reticently, in long difficult words, to Carlotta Moi.

"Oh, she's always complaining, that one," she answered sharply, confidently. I remembered the fluid, enfolding voice of my Elide, who had never intimidated me; never, as Carlotta did now, face to face with my problem.

I let Carlotta Moi walk all over me.

I realized also that the accounts were not always right and among her things in my bedroom—yes, I rummaged among them—I found Elide's savings book.

Carlotta Moi never used the closet in Elide's room. As long as she slept in my room, she kept all her things in two suitcases under the bed, and her clothes were hung up to air. She did her work in silence, without singing or whistling, and she wore shoes with rubber soles. She told me complicated stories I didn't always understand. When my mother ate out, Carlotta sat in my mother's place at the table while I ate, and, always touching and adjusting the braid on her head, she spoke in that distinct way of hers, addressing me as "dear Miss Marzia." I was embarrassed at having to eat in front of her, as she occasionally took a cherry from the fruit bowl and spat the seed into my dirty plate after she had shifted the fruit around in her mouth among her sparse teeth. Sometimes her serving at table became simply a long standing before me, which lasted throughout my meal—I had prepared a book beside me in vain—until she went back into the kitchen again.

She would tell me: "The lady where I worked before said I had grown fat, too fat, and she was afraid I had something wrong with me. Then she took me to a doctor, Doctor L'Asaro, or D'Asaro, I don't know, and this doctor wanted to examine me, and I told them nobody was going to look at me, and he, he was so disagreeable, he may have been a doctor, and a smart one, too, I don't say he wasn't, but he was disagreeable, and he tells me that if my things don't come regular, it was an ailment or else a baby, and he wanted to see. Well, to make a long story short, I left that lady's house, because there are some things I won't let anybody do to me. But I tell you, my dear Miss Marzia, my legs here, the thighs, were so fat I couldn't walk, and with the hot weather, they rubbed together and got all red, and it hurt. . . . All the same, I didn't eat, because there wasn't any food, with the war and all. . . ."

I didn't understand much of her stories, but when I had finished eating, thinking of her fat legs—she had shown them to me and I couldn't get them out of my sight—I helped her clear away the dishes that were left on the table and then I came back to remove the cloth. I hardly ever spoke to her, except when it was indispensable, and, when I spoke, she would stare at my mouth with a grimace.

"MARZIA, make this phone call for me," my mother said. "Speak softly, slowly, and I'll be listening to you. Call Peppino and tell him I have the injunction ready, but now I have to go out. If he can come by this evening after seven, we'll look at it together. Go ahead. Go on. You know the number."

I knew Peppino's number, of course. As I went toward the big desk, my heart started pounding. I wasn't angry with my mother because I knew she inflicted that torture on me to get me into the habit of speaking. I took a deep breath, slowly, as I dialed the number, hoping it would be busy, that my desire would make it so. It wasn't, however, and the bell rang. One ring, two, three. My head measured the seconds of those rings in all their length, tangible, palpable.

"He doesn't answer," I said, again with a ray of hope.

"Wait a little longer. He must be in."

Suddenly he answered and I said "Hello" before I had realized it.

"Hello. Yes? Who is it? Hello, hello, hello?" he said from the other end of the wire, and his impatience gave way to resignation, just as I began to fear he would hang up again. I gulped in spasms, afraid I wouldn't make it in time; my mother was looking at the floor.

Finally: "Y-yes . . . hello . . . This is Mar-Marzia B-Bri . . ."

"Oh, Marzia, it's you. What is it?" the voice answered, now friendly, calm: he wanted to make me feel calm, too.

28

"Y-yes . . . I wanted to s-say that M-Mamma has to g-go out, and . . ." And then it went rather well, or else it went badly, and I writhed in the chair, toying with the telephone wire and with the pencils while I glimpsed my mother making broad gestures, meaning: Slowly, go slowly, take it easy. . . . But I went on at the same speed, blocking, letting it come out as it came; it would always be like this, and besides Peppino was an old friend and he knew how I spoke and a pause more or less made no difference. And if instead of Peppino I had had to call someone else, a stranger, and I had first deceived myself that he might not notice . . . so much the worse. Now she'll leave, I was thinking meanwhile of my mother. She'll leave and I'll be alone, and I'll go out on the balcony.

I LOOKED AT PEOPLE while they talked. I followed the anatomy of others' speech; I felt I could grasp the physical aspect of thought, see the nerves twisting and twisting like wires until they succeeded in moving the tongue—that horrid muscle— without obstacles, without the need of further, conscious commands. Fascinated, I watched mouths move; disgust at this autopsy mounted in me, but I went on. I thought my block was there, somewhere in the middle, between thought and tongue, along the nerve wires. I know what I want to say, I thought, I have the words ready. I want to say, "I'm busy." But I know that "I'm" won't come out, because it's behind a mountain. Lots of breath won't suffice to overcome that mountain, to say "I'm." So I compromise, which makes me angry. I say, "Now I'm," which is ugly—the hell with it— but it will come out. I think, I think and I say, in one blurt,

"Now I'm so busy." There, that "so" wasn't prepared, I hadn't decided to say it, and yet it came out on its own, smooth and unsuspected. Precisely because it wasn't prepared, I say to myself. But is that enough? What about poems? I don't trip over poems. Because I know I know them? But "I'm busy" was something I knew well. Then it's because this isn't poetry, or music, or rhythm, or melody. . . . Speak softly, slowly. From now on I'll speak softly, very softly, I won't let anything upset me. There, I'll begin now, at the fruit shop. I'll go in, I'll speak slowly, enunciating, as if I were speaking another language. I'll be content, immediately conceited inside. The clerk doesn't know how I usually speak and won't be surprised that I speak like this, I tell myself. Of course, there's nothing strange about it, I tell myself, lots of people speak slowly; and people like it too, it's restful.

"Do you have any change?" the fruit seller's wife asks. "I can't change that bill, I really can't," she adds, with the splendid abundance, the squandering of words by people who talk. They were unexpected, the woman's words. This surprise releases me from my resolve before I'm aware of it; suddenly I feel as if I were on vacation; I drop the pure, distinct recitation of a moment before.

I answer, "Change? No, I'm sorry, I don't have enough. I don't." Well. I spoke well. But what's the use? The next time I'll be back where I was. I can't keep a promise to myself; I have no character. I'll never achieve anything, never.

> But as his eyes upon that fair face gazed,
> He pity felt, and killed him not.

Those verses, how beautiful they were! I sought them within me and repeated them to myself, with tears in my throat.

And one day I read in De Sanctis that in a class full of young people there is always an irresistible emotion at the reading of that passage. Then I wept with joy. "I'm like the others, I'm like all the others," I said, and I was happy.

MY GRANDMOTHER DIED in those years when we had Carlotta Moi and Elide no longer understood anything. Some furniture from the house in Via Pietro Cavallini came to us; other pieces went to distant relatives; but not the big wardrobe with the "clothes to be sewn." That stayed there, in its room.

My mother called me into her bedroom that day, and her hair was all white, short, falling at either side of her head like two tired wings as she rummaged in the upper drawer of the bureau. She took a box from some ancient tissue paper, opened it and, without removing the brooch it contained, gave it to me, saying, "This is yours. It belonged to your grandmother."

AT THE LICEO there was a dark girl in my class whose name was Luciana, but she called herself Lucia, with the accent on the "u." She owned a fragment of a comb, a big reddish comb with broad teeth, which she used often and called "Stump."

"There I lend Stump to Franca for a moment, and Pagani starts grumbling at once and makes me give it to him. Imagine! Franca and I were giggling like a pair of idiots!"

She always said words like "grumble" instead of "speak" and "giggle" instead of "laugh," and everybody was called

31

that idiot or that nut. She loved her words, and I loved them, too.

"Will you phone me today?" she said, and then she was the one who phoned me, asking me to meet her. So I left my homework, which had suddenly become scant and easy, and ran to the meeting, ready to wait, rather than be waited for. Lucia was witty and carefree, she had lots of friends and she talked about them, but I never saw them. She amused me, she excited me. I was proud that she liked to be with me. I imitated her style, though I didn't dare assume all her words, and, as she spoke fast, I began to speak fast, too, in long sentences, all in one breath, often without halting, or with very brief halts, short blocks that I angrily overcame. I was all agitated, in a sweat. With her, I blocked seriously, badly, only when she asked me to tell her something.

"*Avez-vous de l'argent?*" Lucia would say, and with fifty or eighty lire we went to the Cinema Eden or the Cola di Rienzo or the Palestrina, and during the film she nudged me or grabbed my arm at the exciting moments. We came back from the movies, arm in arm, hurrying, speaking again, and I would walk her home, though she lived beyond my house, behind Castel Sant'Angelo, and then I would come home again, all excited, unable to do anything but wander around the rooms, thinking of her, in her warm home, rich—as I imagined it—in brothers and carpets. And I dreamed of a real intimacy with her, even more real and affectionate, and she would speak to me of my handicap, even making fun of it. I longed for this. Instead, she never did anything of the kind.

I spoke easily with Luciana. When at school, as I was being questioned, I forced myself to think of her, present there, in order to speak well; it didn't work. When I was examined, it was always torment for the whole class: that was what I felt. Remembering the days of the lovely memorized poems in the ginnasio, which did really come out without a halt, I thought of memorizing a first sentence of the lesson. "Italy was united. Still, it was not the Italy that Mazzini had dreamed of. . . ." I remember. I had hoped that, after the confident beginning, the rest would go well. It didn't. I realized I would have had to memorize the whole chapter. I could never do that. I aimed at the end of the school year with the certainty that during the summer—the vast summer —I would learn to be calm, to speak well, "breathing the way singers breathe."

"Like singers," my mother said, "you must learn to breathe like singers." And she took me to Professor Marchetti.

He was in Via Cavour, one of those huge, livid buildings at the lower end. For the first time my mother didn't insist I speak on coming in, introducing myself. I looked around, my lips clenched. The professor was small and he spoke distinctly, a bit like Carlotta Moi, and he explained to my mother the course which "the little lady," namely me, would be following. Then he took us into a room full of boys, with the strong odor of male classrooms; he called on one of the boys, then another and another.

"Tell the lady what your name is, and how old you are," he said, and the boy, after taking a breath, answered slowly, preparing each syllable in his mouth, as if he were cooling off a hot meatball.

"Now let's hear the little lady," the professor said, and led us into a waiting room. At a small desk, he gave me something to read. I opened my mouth for the first time. And I read; I read quickly, very well, though without understanding anything of what I was reading so easily. I finished, and in my mother's eyes I saw triumph and also gratitude; behind that sad little desk she seemed young to me, and helpless.

33

We left, and on the stairs she pressed my hand as she hadn't done for a long time. "You've given me a present," she said, and I was so moved I couldn't answer. "You see? You can do it, and you don't have to talk like those poor children. He gave me his schedule and said he'll be expecting you. He'll have a long wait."

She skipped down the steps like a girl. Then she gave me some money: a thousand lire, the largest, most embarrassing amount I'd ever had. It was like stolen money to me.

"AND HOW'S THE GENETRIX? Amusing herself with her criminals?" Luciana asked me. "She's a real woman, all right. She must make plenty of shekels. I hear she was the first woman lawyer in Rome. You didn't tell me that."

One afternoon I was on my way home, and from the landing I could already hear laughter, talking, in the study. I went to my room, thinking of nothing, but soon I heard the glass door open and words and laughter approach.

"Here she is, in her lair! So this is how you forget your engagements! It's a good thing we heard you come in, because you . . . you weren't giving us a thought!"

My mother was with her, with Lucia; my mother, who never came out of her study in the afternoon. Bright and smiling, she said to her, "Make her study. And teach her to think sharp, to draw conclusions and to be less easygoing. To know what she wants, to have a will of her own."

When she left the two of us alone—"She's so nice," Lucia said, running "Stump" through her long hair, hanging from her bent head. The comb made a sharp, electric sound.

We studied until late, and, as she was leaving, Lucia

34

opened the study door, stuck her head in and said " 'Bye." My mother was with a client, but she turned, smiled and said " 'Bye," raising her hand. My mother never said " 'Bye." I never opened the door of her study unless she called me.

"I really like her," Luciana added at the door, again with "Stump" in her hair.

I STUDIED WELL with Lucia. While we kept the book open before us, the excitement of conversation wasn't stirred up. She followed the text with her eyes as I read fluently. Then she would repeat the words while I listened; but it often happened that I interrupted and went on, following the notion of the page without trouble, its thought becoming one with mine, as if I were one with the book. Then, at night, in bed, I reflected on our hours of study, and the information I had absorbed seemed something I would be able to give back, smooth, identical; indeed, I felt it would be wrong to go and look at the texts again or repeat them, running the risk of destroying the equilibrium.

But if my mother stopped in the doorway, or if I imagined a listener—who might be the examiner or just Lucia herself—my fine reading stopped, and it was possible for me to resume only after an operation of mental detachment, the shifting of my intention from the text's subject to its form, a recitation of sentences I wouldn't then understand, as I had done at Professor Marchetti's.

At night, in bed, I always looked at the picture on the wall next to me. It was of a courtyard. I looked at the little railing of a neat balcony, the rain pipe clean and bodiless, the cage on the little balustrade which was partly hidden by the window, so the presence of the bird, which couldn't be seen, was uncertain. Time and again I thought of that little bird, who couldn't be seen in the picture. I felt myself in that courtyard, and I imagined, beyond those windows, the apartment in Via Pietro Cavallini.

"SEE WHAT YOU CAN DO about Monday night; we're having a few people in."

Inviting friends to dinner was a novelty, something that started after the war. They were new, noisy people, violently involved in politics; no longer the silent women and the smiling men of the beach at Ostia, so many years before. What had happened to them? The only one left was Peppino, who, however, never appeared at our dinner parties. I prepared myself for them with anguish, and was always defeated. My mother never made any comment, afterward, on the outcome of the evening. She went off to bed, tired and silent, while I helped Carlotta Moi dry the dishes and glasses.

"THERE ISN'T MUCH TIME now before this diploma," my mother said. "Get busy, work, work hard. Stick with Lucia. Do what she does; she's a smart girl. And get rid of your doubts, if you have any. But do you? I don't think you even have them."

I was trembling; what doubts was she talking about? She wanted me to enroll in law school, I was sure of that. And through long, sleepless nights, lying immobile in bed, I told myself this was the misunderstanding, the error rooted between us always, since before I was born, when my mother had wanted a boy. The error that had grown up with me as I went to eat chicken at my grandmother's, who made my dresses with Maria the dressmaker, whereas she bought me shoes with laces; the misunderstanding that had swollen between us as Elide died limply in her bed. She had wanted me like herself, more herself than she was. And it was right, I decided. But I was silent, then, even inside. I was very tired, I believe, and I had lost all elasticity except in the studying that filled my days. When I wasn't bent over my books, I was in a state of dumb stupor, or I thought, I'm still in time to fail. Yes, and then what? I saw nothing before me except endless examinations.

"Let's take a little stroll," Lucia said. "My head's about to burst. A stroll along the Tiber and then you can walk me home." We rushed down the stairs, in the late summer afternoon. We walked along the Tiber under the plane trees, under the flowering locusts, to Ponte Margherita, to Ponte Vittorio, then back again. She talked all the time, and I talked, too, nonsense, things of no importance. We laughed, because we were tired of studying and wanted to laugh. I walked her to Castel Sant'Angelo and then I turned back toward home. In my solitude afterward, at the rhythm of my own footsteps, my silence swelled within me and pressed against me, pounding, painful. I walked faster then, and the enormous, shapeless silence within me grew, mounted, became a scream hammering at my ears and throat while the sidewalk became gigantic, as if it were coming closer and closer to my sight. Then—sooner, later—the scream collapsed, became small, a pitiful moan. In it, little words, still limp, were formed: Little, little, poor me, poor me. I whimpered like a baby. Poor me, that's what she wants, but what can I do, what can I do, poor me, she wants that, she wants me to become like that, like her, and it's not possible, I can't do it, I can't, poor me. Poor me, lawyers argue, they argue and talk all the time, they talk and talk. And I could see, with a dream sensation, chains of entangled words, forests of words, forests of sentences erect before me.

I had sat on a low bench and I was dragging my sandals through the gravel, pushing it aside, and I looked at the bared ground, the brownish dust that was collecting under the nails of my big toes. My goodness, what dirty feet, I said, and I thought of death. I looked at my toenails with the dust, feeling the contact of the gravel against my bare toes; I saw myself taking lots and lots of pills in a row—two bottles, twelve to the bottle, I calculated—with a big glass of water; I felt in the palms of my hands how I would break each tablet into two or even three pieces, because it's irksome to swallow them whole, and they leave a dry feeling in your throat. I dragged my sandals in the dust a little longer; other images came—or else they didn't come and I was left with the pills— and after a while I had finished with the dirt for that day, and I felt better. I got up from the bench, I headed for home. I passed the rest of the little garden and Via Marianna Dionigi serenely, less tired, and now it seemed to me I would be able to say everything right out, from now on, forever, because all my blocks had vanished in the screaming silence that had filled me.

Lucia was more and more at home, before and after the exams, and my mother invited her to eat with us. And so at the table we talked, with animation. After the exams, we got into the habit of going to the swimming pool. Lucia introduced me to her friends, and often my mother came too, always talking with her, laughing, revealing her gums. She told

Lucia things about her life I had never known, about the war years when she fabricated false documents and then was in Regina Coeli prison. I looked at her thighs, flabby and white now; her breasts, mortified in her old black wool bathing suit, as they always were in her mannish suits; her white feet flung out, flat, on the tiles by the pool. I knew all that about her, but that she should offer it, with her lighthearted stories, there, in the sun of the terrace, to Lucia and her friends, offended me. My gaze became absent, and then she called me back, showing her gums, speaking to me, but not directly. "Shall we tell her? This snail without a shell?" she would say, with an accomplice-smile, to Lucia, and Lucia would laugh, too, but she would also defend me a bit, only she, calmly looking at me and saying Why? Finally I would doze off on the tiles of the terrace, while they went on laughing.

Then Lucia went off for her summer holiday where she would rediscover old friendships and memories. My mother said good-bye to her at the door; and when Lucia had gone down the stairs, she said: "Are you staying here? You can't expect me to take you away. Yes, we might be able to go for a few days perhaps, but you'll get bored with me. Don't you have any friends, someplace to go, anywhere; doesn't Lucia want you? Go somewhere else then, go and meet other people; I'll give you the money. Do you want some money?"

I stayed in Rome, alone with her and with Carlotta, who was now about to go away, a prospect that relieved me and also caused me a subtle anguish.

For two weeks, without Lucia, I walked along the walls, I sat in the little gardens in Piazza Cavour, I passed under the windows of Via Pietro Cavallini which now had different curtains. And, always, my mother's desire for me to enroll in law school swelled within me; when I set my feet on the slabs of the sidewalk, avoiding the cracks as I had done when a little girl, when with maniacal care I stepped from one stone to another, never touching two at once.

I saw it again before my eyes, that pavement, even at night, in bed; and I gulped nervously at the anguished image of an infinite expanse of words stretching into a desperate future made up of exam after exam. I walked alone again, and I happened to feel beside me Giorgina Riva, the little girl who was perhaps sick, my companion in the ginnasio, whom I had never seen since. At first her company was silent, inspired by some memory or association; then she returned often to my imagination and became the mute listener to whom I said little, trivial things, light words, out of a desire not to feel alone any more, comments on what I saw in a shopwindow. Then I started going out in order to meet her, her ghost, in the street. At the beginning, in fact, I never brought her home, and I never talked with her on the steps. Feeling her at my side in the street, I would return to my obsessive thought. "You see?" I would say to her, "she wants that, but what can I do? No, she's never told me, but I know it. Not that I want to do nothing, I really like studying, or at least I'm used to it, it's what I've always done, after all. . . . Yes, I have an idea about something I'd like to study, but . . . Yes, I think I'd succeed, I like the subject, and besides it's something easy, I think, you can do it without . . . without too much contact with other people. . . . I don't know, something easy, I mean. . . ." I didn't say a subject that requires the least possible talking. Not even to her, who didn't exist, who was myself, not even then did I say it. "Yes, an easy subject, that's all. . . . Yes, I'll have to tell her. Yes, tonight. One day's as good as another, you say. Yes . . . You always say everything to everybody, don't you? You say tonight. Now I'll explain to you. I'll go home and I'll find her in the study, beyond the glass door. . . . No, the glass is opaque, but you can see all the same, or at least I'm used to it and I can understand when somebody's in there, and besides you hear the voices. I would have to wait for her to come out. Then we're at the table. At the table it's more difficult. . . ."

Soon I came to dislike having that invented Giorgina Riva with me, and, precisely because she was an invention, I couldn't dismiss her or ignore her. Slowly I sank into a glum silence. And then she became an obsession, a persecution. Giorgina Riva climbed the stairs with me, she kept me company everywhere. And she was the one who wanted to talk with me about that thing, about my future work. I realized I would have to tell my mother of my decision to study chemistry and not law right away. Right away, and unexpectedly. Unexpectedly for myself, above all; and it was essential that I conclude everything before Lucia's return, which still seemed remote to me. I would be bold, display boldness. I would talk, I would be listened to. It was a perfect plan because from the moment I told her my decision, I would be free to do what I wanted and, not only that, free forever in my speech. Like the others: like Giorgina Riva the talker, like Lucia the chatterbox. Already Giorgina's ghost was growing faint, driven off by my decision; already Lucia was becoming negligible.

So certain and radiant was the fruit of my decision that the price to be paid—a few words to my mother—seemed very little to me. I dwelt on my endless future as an easy talker. Let's see: "Mamma, you know what I've decided?" No, that's a mistake. I mustn't prepare a little speech; I must catch it off guard. I mustn't allow four miserable words to . . . I must just do it, like that, at an ordinary moment. . . . Ah, how wonderful!

I was really happy. I went to Piazza Cavour to my bench,

I shifted the gravel and the dust with my sandals, and I smiled at my dirty toes. I still had ten days before Lucia's return and I enjoyed myself by jiggling in my pocket the key to all my problems. "I'll have those pockets of yours sewn up!" I remembered. And I smiled.

So, sure of myself, in lazy expectation of the mysterious impulse of a certain "ordinary" moment, I let time and the days go by blissfully, still blocking and halting, with Carlotta Moi, with my mother, with the newsvendor. Feeling almost joy, a kindly compassion—so it seemed to me—for my poor handicap, unaware its days were numbered.

I heard her on the telephone, Saturday evening.

"Tomorrow morning, yes. I'll catch the express at eight. I'll see you Wednesday or Thursday."

I had to speak to her at once or she would leave and in the meantime Lucia would arrive. Panic-stricken, I felt a victim, defrauded. It was normal for her not to have told me. She always told me at the last moment when she was leaving, and often with a "What? Didn't you know?" which amused and almost moved me at her slight embarrassment. I saw our evening before us, with her voiceless; Carlotta grumpy; the cat, the only creature to whom all three of us spoke gladly; and string beans, poached eggs. Of course, I could have spoken. But now I felt deceived, and from my position as victim I knew very well that I would take a cowardly advantage of myself.

Still I did say, "Mamma, you know . . ."

I said it in the hall, a stupid ordinary moment. She didn't hear me and shut the bathroom door after her.

"Oh, to hell with it!" I shrugged with a nasty grimace of victorious resentment, cowardly content already. And so I had given up.

"SAY HELLO to Lucia for me," she said again, before leaving. "Find some company for yourself, go to the beach, you're as yellow as a squeezed lemon."

I remember that whole Sunday, the sirocco coming on top of the summer sultriness. Carlotta had left me alone in the house; the blinds and windows were closed to trap what little coolness there was. I went to Mass at San Rocco, as I liked to, and the bridge with the swirling dust and the little fruit of the plane trees already withered in the corners seemed longer, as it always did on Sunday. The church was almost empty; the cobblestones burned beneath my sandals. I came home with my mouth shut; I was mute, and, I believe, not unhappy, made lazy by the sirocco and by the expectation of nothing. My anguish at her wish, placated by my determination to speak to her, didn't return. Speak to her: I no longer knew when, how or if I would. Lucia's return—she had written me an exuberant letter—was a deadline to which I still attributed a decisive importance. But I didn't look beyond that deadline.

I came back into the cool, rotten odor of the courtyard; I climbed the dark stairs also gritty with the sirocco dust. The cat spoke to me and I didn't choose to answer him, I remember, even at his nuzzling when I had flung myself down on the bed. I ate an enormous salad and little else. Then—I felt I was breaking a rule—I opened the blinds and went onto the study balcony where I weeded the plants, added some earth, watered them, rearranged the pots. I was more relaxed afterward. I shut the blinds again and dusted the study; I picked up some leaves that had blown in. The cat, stretched out in

43

the middle of the hall, looked at me through half-closed eyes. Carlotta came home earlier than usual, sooner than I would have liked, so I went out again, and in Piazza Cavour there were stands selling grapes from Maccarese and people coming back from the beach. I went home for supper a little late and went to bed to read.

And so three more days of waiting for nothing went by; I visited half-deserted offices on errands for my mother and I typed up some things she had left for me; I had done this forever, more or less, "So you can learn," she said. She didn't say it was really useful to her; I would have preferred that.

Lucia's return was as I had feared: exciting and unpleasant. Eating bread and butter, she asked me, "Well, what are we going to do? Sign up for law, both of us?" And I sensed, behind her words, an errand that perhaps wasn't there.

"Not I," I said, almost without realizing it. It had come out on its own, like water, after all.

She ignored me and continued, "We'll sign up for law and we'll have fun. We'll study together; we'll get practical experience with your mother. Not bad, having a law office like hers behind you."

"Not I," I said, with effort this time. And I went on, ready to stammer, "I don't want to enroll in law. I've thought it over, and it's not for me. I'm going to study something else."

"My God, listen to her! What do you want to do then? Study literature and be a schoolteacher? Good heavens! With eyeglasses, a saggy bottom and bad breath. Children, be quiet, or I'll send for the principal," she added, cawing, and peering over imaginary lenses.

"No. I'm studying chemistry."

44

"Chemistry? Well. Oh, study what you like. I'm doing law."

"It's right for you. I'm glad . . . in fact . . . if you come to the office here. . . ." I said, relieved, embarrassed, blushing, since now it seemed ridiculous for me to be hospitable when I certainly didn't feel I was the mistress of the house.

"Well, I should think so. So long, Miss Chemist. I've got to run. They're waiting for me. 'Bye. Here's a kisslet."

She kissed me on the forehead and went out. I ran and shut myself in the bathroom, even though I was alone in the house, filled with anger and relief. "I needn't have said anything, I needn't have said anything," I repeated. Lucia wasn't the one to whom I had to speak; I had to say it to her. Now it's useless, and I won't be able to tell her, and I have to, or else Lucia will.

So, as I had foreseen, without admitting it to myself, in the days past, everything was deflated and ruined. Still I told myself, "But she doesn't know, I have time to tell her on my own, and then I'll be able to talk, forever." I said this aloud, but I knew it wasn't true.

When she came back I didn't say anything. And the next day, at the table, when Lucia was with us, she bit into a peach and looked out of the window, as she said, "So I hear you've chosen the stinks."

At first I didn't understand, not even that she was talking to me.

"I'm talking to you, Miss Chemistry Major. I hear you want to shut yourself up with retorts and alembics, and produce yellow steam. That way you'll become even more yellow yourself."

Caught off guard and so awkwardly, I felt my stomach

leap; and yet it was clear to me that the blow I had dealt her was harder, less bearable than I had feared. Words jammed my throat: No, no, wait. . . . Only the No, no came out . . . and nothing else, while Lucia's napkin ring spun around her finger.

Then, after the silence, my mother got up and stopped beside me for a moment. She clasped my shoulder with her big, steady hand. "It doesn't matter," she said. "You're right. Don't think I disapprove. I do approve. Only, I'm sorry."

That "I'm sorry" wounded me with sudden heat.

At night I went to her room and stopped in the doorway, my teeth clenched, my tongue thick in my mouth. Her silvery head was on the pillow and her glasses with their big frames, like a man's, cast a shadow on her temple, and another shadow made a dark hollow beneath her cheekbone. She was reading her thriller rapidly as always, holding it folded back in her stubby hand. She flipped the page, leaving it free, and giving the book a shake in the air. I stood at the door for a long time while she went on reading.

"What is it?" she asked then, without voice.

I went to her bed, not speaking, and tears burst my swollen chest. "I'm sorry" burned within me, and I sobbed, "I'm sorry."

She put down the book and her hand moved to my hair, while her toneless, night voice said slowly: "Silly, my silly girl, don't worry, you'll always have me behind you, as long as the old carcass holds up. You're all I have. Naturally, I could have been of more help to you, but I was expecting it and I should have expected it. I would have left you the practice and instead it'll go to the first Lucia who knows her way around a bit. You're worth a lot more, mind you. I want you to know that. Don't forget it. You're worth a hundred Lucias. Don't think I don't understand you. You're afraid of talking and that's how you see my profession mostly. What you've chosen is also a good career, but there will be exams connected with it, too, and you'll have to speak. What can I say to you: Darling, don't worry? You'll see, though: if you want to do it and you like it—because, first of all, you must like it—if you want to do it and you like it, I'm sure you can and I'll encourage you. But tell me, tell me . . ." and she raised my chin to look into my face, as she had when I was a child, and I shut my swollen eyes . . . "tell me: you'll still make a phone call to the courthouse for me now and then, won't you? I can still ask that of you? You think I don't know what an effort it was for you to make calls for me and go on errands; you must have cursed me time and again, but I wanted to help you and then . . . well, yes, I still hoped you would follow me. Tell me: do you remember your father? I've asked myself over and over. He was like you, you know, in lots of things. Very much like you. Very much."

That hour has left a memory I cannot explore further. I went to my bed in the dark, after I had turned off her light, and that time she didn't finish her book. I remained awake under the picture with the roofs, in the dark, weeping now and then with remorse and with joy.

MY FIRST YEAR at the university has left a brief memory made of light. The great light of the paths still with young trees then, and the nearby streets: broad, smooth, in an urban dimension so different from that of my dark sidewalks thick with odors; the great wall of wisteria of the General Hospital.

The hours of the day, which I divided between my old streets and the new, were nourished on an adventurous, thrilling contrast. I stayed at the university as late as possible, and there for the first time I felt truly different. I went under the pergola in front of the chemistry department, content with the future I felt within myself, all ready. And so I walked along the broad white edge of those sidewalks, reciting the old poems; when it rained, under my umbrella I sang. Only I didn't feel alone, unobserved; I felt observed, followed, accompanied. Accompanied by whom? Not by Giorgina Riva: I had left her on the black cobbles around my house; not by Lucia, whom I had also left in my neighborhood, actually in my own home. Lucia spent a lot of time with my mother, and this made me happy. I was happy to stand in line at the dean's door and the bursar's office, among talkative boys and girls with their hair neatly combed, and those anodyne places for me became the fantastic seat of the young, vital world I wanted to feel mine: my world. I didn't think that the life of those boys and girls went on in houses, places, streets of Rome unknown to me, and while the gray bursar's office was illuminated for me by them, it was for them an indifferent, ugly place, quickly forgotten.

I went to my classes, always reciting and observing my-self, present to myself among the others, the friend of those who didn't look at me, silent with a thousand implications, too affable with those who barely greeted me. In reality, I almost never spoke: alone, I spoke in the street; at home, I was silent. And I hardly noticed that I spoke haltingly as I had before, as always. I was pleased with myself, and Softly now, slowly, I said to myself, as if my happy speech were about not to fail me. Soon it would blossom as if from a long incubation: certainly before the June exams, which seemed very far away to me. I dreamed of the laboratory where I would work next year and the smell of hydrogen sulphide which came from behind the chemistry building seemed almost good. Breathing that stink was an enviable confirmation.

At the beginning of the year Lucia had organized a party to celebrate her and my university admittance. I was already going to classes, and she said, "I'm not going to set foot in the university until I've passed the initiation and have my papers. How do you manage? Haven't the older students stopped you?"

"N-no. Why? Should they?"

"Annetta, you hear her? Where have you been all your life?" she said, turning again to me. Annetta was my mother, whom she now called by her first name. And that name, which I so seldom heard used, seemed to me on her lips something defenseless, shameless.

"What did I tell you? We'll have to do everything ourselves. Annetta, come, we'll arrange it all."

"What have I got to do with it?"

"Well, if you'll lend your house, I think you'll have something to do with it. I'll bring the old folks."

"How many of you will there be?"

"There'll be . . . two, five, six, eight. . . . Oh, not so many, maybe ten. Ah, unless Marzia brings someone. Who're you going to bring, Marzia? After all . . ."

"Why . . . nobody, I think."

Silence. I remember that silence.

And I remember my mother dancing, laughing, drinking with those boys and girls, with that "younger generation" while through my pitiless looking at her, true pity for her filled me. The words she had spoken to me that night from her bed had become a memory almost unreal, arcane.

I HAD THOUGHT of chemistry as a wordless subject: I had imagined a great field of symbols and formulas, without sentences; I had visualized myself at exams—me, the blackboard, the chalk—without the anguish of speaking. It wasn't like that. I had studied hard, and in June I took three important exams, horribly blurted out. I emerged from those days exhausted, speaking very badly. I knew that with some rest I would improve, it wouldn't last long; then, in October, it would be even worse.

Meanwhile it was summer. My mother was wearing her ancient canvas shoes, the ones she used to wear when we went to Ostia. She said to me: "Will you come with me one of these days? I go to the river, something they would never let me do when I was a little girl like you. Come. I'll introduce you to some new people, very nice. People who mean something. Will you do me this honor?"

"Yes," I answered, and I would have liked to say, "Wonderful!" Our reciprocal embarrassment increased just when occasions and our own wishes should have brought us closer together. When we were alone, all the things I had thought out, prepared, remained in me, stifled by silences that became more and more ponderous. The same thing happened to her; then I felt I was her daughter.

We went down the little steps to the bank of the Tiber. On the barge we met a woman who had been in prison with my mother; she was wearing a tiny, brightly colored, two-piece suit on her brown, fifty-year-old body, dried by the sun. She was stretched out on the warm wood, with two pads of cotton on her eyes, the same ones every time, and the only living thing about her was her enormous, ugly teeth and her thick, pale tongue, never still. Obsessively, I listened to her soft "r," certain that she had once been ashamed of it, then had accepted it and finally had seized on it furiously.

"Monstwous. Simply monstwous, I tell you. A filthy twick." And her horribly pregnant "r" seemed present even in words that didn't have one. My mother laughed, irresistibly and a bit ashamed, and at the end of each burst of laughter, as if she wanted to break it off or hide it, she added a "So," awkward and meaningless, though I don't think she was aware of it.

I didn't listen to what the two women said to each other, but as my senses were heightened by the sun, by the immobility, by the searing footsteps of the men on the barge, by the smell of the wood, by being so low and near the river, whose odor I could smell and whose flow I could feel, wrinkles and smooth eddies over the murky depths, my impotence panted in secret. Alone with those two, who talked and talked, clever, voluble, violent, in all that flow—and if I opened my eyes, the clouds sped dizzyingly by—I groped desperately in the anguished stagnancy within me. They talk, they say whatever they want. I can't. And from my inability to speak, inertia rose and invaded all my faculties, even to the very source of thought, to the void. I woke finally as if from a whirling sleep, from a drug, to resume habitual acts farther from thought than anything else.

That summer, I slept in the afternoon. Out of boredom especially, as never before. Then I did the exercises recommended in my stoichiometry textbook, convinced I was doing them properly, but when I looked up the results, I had got them wrong. I watered the plants, I went out, walked to Ponte Margherita, took a long stroll along the walls, alone. Empty, I didn't dream, I didn't speak.

Lucia came back from a trip and went down to the river with us one morning. She was silent the whole time, dangling her round, dark legs over the water close below. When we started for home, my mother took Lucia and me by the arm—when she and I were alone, we never walked like that—and climbed the steps, breathless, walking on in silence. Between the two of them there was silence, too.

At sunset Lucia came into my room, where I was studying. "Let's go out," she said, and looked at the books on the shelf; she knew them all. We went down the stairs slowly, without speaking. Then, in the street, but only after a while, she asked, "Who's that Viviana? What did she tell you about her?" I said she had been in prison with my mother, and that was all I knew.

"Yes, your mother, for all her superior wisdom, sometimes is like a little girl. Has she come to your house, too? Does she visit you at home, eh?" I could feel her burning eyes beneath her disheveled hair, even though I was looking at the ground. I swallowed several times. "N-no . . . I don't know. . . . N-not to the h-house."

It was as if Lucia hadn't listened to me, as if she were walking alone, had forgotten me, though she was still dragging me by the arm. She looked at the ground, shaking her long smooth hair, so I couldn't see her face. We hadn't spoken for the whole length of Via Pietro Cavallini, we were at the end of Via Gioacchino Belli. I had a stone in my sandal and I left it there; but then I said, "Excuse me a moment," and stopped, leaning against the base of the wall. I took the stone out, then drank casually at the fountain. She had stopped mechanically, without saying anything; she stared straight ahead at the street, her mouth clenched. We turned along the Tiber and came back to my house without Lucia's speaking again.

"Well, so long," she said to me then, and, "Don't worry," in a hoarse, waking-up voice.

I climbed the stairs alone, with a feeling of wicked amusement at Lucia's jealousy, which, however, aroused no wonder in me. Then Lucia didn't turn up for a while.

AUTUMN CAME with the colored signs and lights reflected on the wet asphalt, flowering among the crests of the trees, which turned emerald green at evening. The boys who worked in the dairy shops and cafés, their white aprons tied over their hips, stood in the doorways scattered with sawdust, their dazed eyes on the sidewalks, where the fallen sawdust stuck to the soles of the passers-by, becoming a felted mud. I walked among silent sensations; coming home I breathed aromas.

I ran into Lucia with some others. She made a fuss over me as if she were older than me. . . . "Say, everybody, this is where my little friend lives. It would be a sin not to put her to work in our waiting-line project. Little one, Marchetti will instruct you in the art of running the box office blockade Saturday for tickets to the De Sabata concert Sunday afternoon. I'll call everybody and wake you up, and I'll come for the second shift." Then there was a swirl of good-byes: strange young hands waving. And so I was to stand in line for the concert at the Teatro Adriano, and to go to the concert with them.

At six in the morning it was dark and the damp air was a little disturbing, the vague smell of burnt leaves at the beginning of winter, the hollow in my stomach, the door of the building still closed, the street and the square empty and wet, with the street lamps burning; going to join the little group, so lively in words, in that desert outside the closed door of the box office, intoxicated me with adventure and pride. By comparison, the bursar's office at the university became nothing.

"You've taken to rising with the lark?" my mother said. "Where are you off to?"

I answered, and these were my first words of the morning, very difficult.

"Ah, good. With friends? I'm glad. Good for you. Concerts? Fine. Meet as many people as you can; don't forget."

Sunday came and we weren't together all the time: two sat on one side and four on the other, in the benches of the top gallery. We met in the intermissions and at first there was nobody for me to stand with because the rest of them had been friends forever and some were going together. I felt a kind of appendage of Lucia's, she who had never had present loves but always legendary, distant ones, and her carefree, electric hair, combed by "Stump." I was grateful that I could laugh with her at the others' horseplay. At the end we met on the steps from the gallery and outside we crossed the square, the street lights in the fog; all, after the long listening, had warm voices, rapid words, laughter.

I went home early, not daring to stay with them. Lucia waved good-bye to me, laughing, opening and closing the fingers of one hand like a baby. *"Au revoir,"* she said. I went to the apartment alone, running up the steps and then, more slowly, repeating to myself the scenes and the words of the others, and my own words, adding to my poor remembered answers rich supplements, now that in my imagination I was infinitely listened to. Or I sang snatches of melody which had come to me on the shore from the symphonic sea I seemed to possess wholly inside me but which immediately, then, drew back, out of reach.

"SO LONG! Where are you going? Do you need any money?" my mother said, without waiting for an answer to her first question. We saw each other little that year, and she said "So long" to me. I had taken the radio into my bedroom and I listened to music till late in the night.

I BECAME an official organic chemistry major and I turned to the laboratory work with my childish enthusiasm for occupations that were chiefly manual. I was proud when I mounted the iron clamps, as my fingers grew stronger, my hands stained and skinned; I was happy then, when I said to Lucia, "Every time I paint my nails, the acetone takes it all off the next morning."

Swelling with joy, I came away from the chemistry building in the evenings when I had lingered until the lights were turned on, and at each little new assignment—you cover the scales, turn off the exhaust of the fan—I enjoyed a new pride. Then on the fog-wet path I walked lightly, full of the day I was leaving behind me, happy at the one coming tomorrow, pleased if I had work to do over Sunday, so I would have to come back to the lab. With all this, I made a deep groove within myself, because I wanted the germ of habit to remain there: so that all would soon become habit and would build that person I dreamed of being.

"QUIET! Tell me what it is," Claudio said, coming from the next room, where he had turned on the radio.

"Wagner," Marco said.

"Brilliant! My grandfather could get that far. . . . But what Wagner?"

Lucia snickered privately, not taking part.

"*Rheingold,*" I said, "the Giants." All eyes were on me.

"Good girl. Go to the head of the class," Claudio said. "And the rest of you, you lazy good-for-nothings; I've been taking you to concerts and the opera for ten years now, and you're still ignorant. Shame, plebeians. Friday, it's no use your coming to hear the Busch Quartet. You wouldn't understand anything, and it's all just snobbery with you. I'll go alone with the little one . . . with Marzia. We'll send the rest of you to the movies."

"Cut it out, intellectual. Want a sandwich? By the way, have you heard? Fausto's coming on Thursday. Shall we put Gianna inside a chocolate Easter egg for him?"

"How? Chloroformed? And there's a certain bald banker you'd also have to bind and gag, at least."

"I ran into Gianna, in Piazza Fiume. She says she's marrying him, that bald banker."

"Let her. I'm not saying this just out of solidarity, but Fausto was better."

"You're overlooking the insignificant fact that he wasn't going to marry her."

"Oh, you bourgeois, thinking only of marriage."

"Listen to who's talking. With that diamond big as an onion on her finger."

That evening I went home in glory, having recognized *Rheingold,* and thinking of Fausto, their friend, who was a real pianist and whom I had never met.

I WAS ALREADY BRIMMING with love: in my steps stolen by the long black sidewalk, in the cold wind against my face, in my just-washed hair flapping as I ran to catch the bus, clasping my books to my breast and the strap of my shoulder bag. I went through the streets around my house, the avenues near the university, along the river, feeling Fausto at my side, a bit taller than me, to my left. I smiled at him. In the sun and under my umbrella, I talked with him. Listen, listen to the rain, smell the grass, the earth. Rain in the city makes all kinds of noises. The wheels of the cars, the drainpipes, the footsteps of the people, the tram tracks. But do you remember rain in the country? And on the beach. We'll go there, one day, to the beach. Silent and broad, rain in the country; vast, so it seems you can hear the little patter of the drops on the leaves nearby, the same but fainter, as it moves farther and farther away, on all sides, fainter and fainter into the distance. And you know what it really is? All the noise is low, from the drops that strike the leaves, perhaps the trees, if they're there, but otherwise it's all low, all on the ground, there, like a carpet of faint, watery noise . . . but noise isn't the right word, let's see what we can say instead: murmur, perhaps, or sound, that's it, sound, that soft thing between the drops and the grass or even the sand, and everything radiating out from it. Oh, I love it! You know what else I think of when it rains? The racket that the rain made on the skylight of my first home, where I was born, in Via Flaminia . . . yes, at the

57

beginning of Via Flaminia, yes. I'll tell you about my childhood a bit, shall I?

An old ruse, I thought to myself, though this didn't diminish the joyous pleasure of telling, of talking to that miraculous ghost. I went home and again, on the stairs, I was with him and I talked with him; ah, how well I talked, smooth, pleasant. I had never talked like this, not even to myself. But passing the glass door—a silent step—I left my Fausto outside. Voices again, in the study, my mother shouting in her shattered voice, poor thing. "Poor thing," I murmured, and I really saw the grim chasm that her life must be, her days without smiles, without the Fausto I had, strolling along the walls. Poor thing. I went into the kitchen, into that old silence, smelling of oilcloth and waxed paper, extended by the tick of Elide's alarm clock with its round numbers and its little legs spread on the cupboard. Carlotta Moi had left and we had a part-time woman in the mornings, no one at night. I dropped a bouillon cube into some water and put it on to boil, to make some soup; I took out the greens, already cooked; and I made an omelet. And I called Fausto back for a little while, as long as I could, as long as I was alone. Then we ate and she said nothing. But often she pushed the plate away.

"I'm not hungry. I don't feel well," she said.

"What can I fix you? Some tea? Something hot?"

"No, I'll take some bicarb later. I treat myself, like cats do, eh, kitty?" she said, stroking the cat, to whom she threw some morsels, as I never dared do, because I had been taught not to feed animals at the table. "Right, kitty?"

This is how our conversation proceeded: through the cat. So it had been for years; and yet, I felt, always present and heavy, our inability to speak to each other. She spoke to the cat when I was present too; I talked to the cat only when

I was alone. Then it was easy; but I didn't say much to him, I stroked him; and afterward, in the street, along the walls, I talked with my Fausto. Poor thing, I thought, she only talks to the cat. And my pity for her was joy, an egoistic physical joy that leaped within me, sang in my throat and made me fly down the dark stairway of the building.

I WOKE UP frightened one night, already aware of what had roused me from sleep. My mother was vomiting. She was in the bathroom with the door open: I knew it from the light and from the sounds. She groaned. I turned to wood in my bed, rigid, but I couldn't pretend I hadn't heard; in fact, I rejected the—instinctive—desire to pretend I hadn't heard, and I quickly got up. I found her bent double, white, her weeping eyes staring at the floor, and she swayed, without looking at me, moaning. I acted before I thought: I wet a cloth, cleaned her, held her up, and she was in my power, she had become small and weak: another person. I stood over her for a long time, hearing her breathing and my own, until she painfully straightened her back. Her eyes closed, and then she looked at me as if from afar. I helped her rinse her mouth; she stood up, clutched her robe with trembling hands. The belt had fallen to the floor; I picked it up, put it around her waist and, as I did, almost embraced her, timidly. We went silently back toward her room, and during that brief, slow walk, she leaned on my arm and her hand clasped mine. The light was burning, and the bed, empty, rumpled, seemed strange and alarming to me, as if I were seeing it like that for the first time. I helped her back into bed and she moaned and seemed to be clearing her throat.

"Do you want something?" I asked her, and she said no, but would I stay with her for a while. "Of course," I answered.

As soon as she was lying down with her eyes closed, when her white hair had regained a halo from the light on her bedside table, I crouched at her feet, alert and, after all, happy. She stirred and said, "You must be cold, put something on," and she pointed to her robe. Even though I wasn't cold, I took the robe and put it over me. I saw her close her eyes again, rested, and after a while she reached out one hand toward me. I suspected she was sleeping already, and I looked at that hand with the dark spots of old age already tangible there, and wanting perhaps to be touched; I looked at it until it became unreal and bodiless, the projection of itself.

I didn't consider her sickness with apprehension; I was only filled with joy at her weakness, her need of me. I thought of her diet for the next day; she would stay in bed and I wouldn't go out but would be there to answer the phone, keep her company, perhaps read something to her. I thought of the room in semidarkness, the shutters closed, perhaps a shaft of sunlight on the floor.

Time went by and she slept, with only an occasional grimace of her serene face and an occasional jerk of the hand that was extended toward me. I thought her shoulder and arm might be cold, and I put them under the blankets, carefully. She sighed in her sleep and I saw again how deep and healthy that sleep was and that the hand stretched toward me, if at first it had had some meaning, now had none. I discovered in myself a greed to tend her and help her. At the first light from the window, I turned out the lamp, folded her robe at the foot of the bed and went out, listening again to her breathing from the silence of the hall. I went back to my now cold bed and with my eyes opened I waited a long time until sleep returned.

I woke up late, remembering everything immediately, and I ran to her. The hall light which I had left burning was turned off, the window was open, the bed empty. She was in the study, at her papers.

"How's everything?" I asked, already shy.

She put down her pen and looked at me quietly for a long moment, diaphanous, and the distance between us was great. "Did you ever see such a thing?" she said then. "I'm turning into a mess."

"Do you want anything? Shall I make you some tea? Why don't you stay in bed?" I said, and already I felt I had struck the wrong note.

"I'm all right. I had some coffee. Don't worry about it. It's over."

In the bathroom my eyes searched in vain for traces of our night.

I STUDIED, and I now had many hours of lab, so the hours at home were few and so separated, one evening from the next, that they seemed almost to blur finally, in habit and boredom. At home I studied, I listened to the radio.

Fausto arrived and, when I saw him at Lucia's, he didn't seem himself, almost a fraud. I came home silent, unable to find words for him along the walls, or for myself.

Seeing him again, I tried to fit his first image to him. And his way of talking and joking only with the others, his ignoring me, I soon turned into an unconscious alibi of his which he enjoyed assuming only with me. A very old game. But with my game I was alone, and I liked it. For a long time my Fausto had been in the music I listened to at night in the darkness, he was in the picture with the courtyard, in my footsteps along the street; the other, the one I wanted to identify with mine, would be with me one day in the line for concert tickets. I waited for him, happy at not knowing when he would come.

He came. We stood side by side. But he had brought something to read, and I read, too, not knowing how to become aggressive and talk, not wanting to. Then someone else came, a friend, and Fausto brightened. He talked with him, for him he abandoned the book. And also, now and then, he talked with me. We walked a little way together and we said something—I didn't say much, and that badly—but talked of nothing, it seemed to me, and as if we were two other people, not the couple I knew. I was ecstatic all the same, and I ran home and flung myself on the bed, all in a tumult. Then nothing was left to me and I called Fausto, Fausto again, but with hollow, stupid rage, my awareness and senses out of control. Or else I wept disconsolately, resentful and silly; then whining.

"HOW ARE YOUR studies going?" my mother asked me one evening in the kitchen, as she sliced herself some mozzarella. "Hurry up and take that degree of yours. Find your place soon. Your own little field, one that's all yours. Think of an Arabic professor at a university. He may not know much Arabic, but he's the only one who knows any, so he has the professorship. You see how many French professors there are, and all of them know French better than he knows Arabic, but they're starving to death. Find your field, specialize, study, work, make some money. You'll need it. You'll need the money . . . unfortunately," she added with a grimace, loosening her belt. "My stomach's swollen," she said then, and looked at it, and stopped eating, and then: "That's enough, I'm going to bed," she said.

I stayed in the kitchen to clear up. I thought with boredom of the same things that she had said to me other times, about finding my place, my little field, and about money. "You'll need money. Not just what you have in your purse, money for concerts, the bus and new shoes. A house takes money, and food, and your chemistry, friends, the concierge's good morning. They don't teach you these things in school, but that's how it is. I've tried to make you understand since you were a child, but I failed. My own fault"—she said. Then I saw her look sad; but this wasn't enough to save her from my pitiless intolerance: intolerance of the truth she was speaking, the truth and the honesty of her personality compared to mine. I had always thrust her words aside with the excuse that the "little field" was an academic phrase that reminded me of Cincinnatus.

I WAS GRADUALLY ACCEPTING the fact that she was not well. Often I heard her get up in the night and walk the floor, or go into the bathroom, and then a great rushing of water. I heard her moan at times and belch, and I got up and went into the hall.

"How are you? Do you need anything?" I would say, with great effort, ashamed at showing I had heard her, at displaying concern.

"No, no, nothing. Go back to bed. I don't want anything. I don't need anything. Go back to bed; you have to study tomorrow. You have work to do. Go on."

I couldn't answer, and I went back to bed. "Shall we call the doctor?" I asked the next morning.

"What do I need a doctor for? My digestion's bad. There are millions of people with indigestion. I'm lucky I've been well until now. Now it's up to you. I haven't seen Lucia lately. What's she doing?"

I told this to Lucia. I told her my mother wasn't well, that she didn't want to have a doctor, that she had asked about her. This is just how I told her, and I immediately realized the grave, fatal sense those words had, lined up in that way. Lucia didn't answer at once, but she frowned. I remembered then that she hadn't come to our house since the time of Viviana, the mornings on the barge in the Tiber. A remote time and, in my memory, foolish. Lucia came.

"How are you, Annetta? What have you been up to?" she said, and even this seemed to me an excessive and serious way of speaking, because my mother was in her study as always, not in bed, ill. I felt a resentment toward Lucia; I saw the scene as one to which deep, premonitory meanings are attributed. At the door, forgetting our old custom of going out together, Lucia said good-bye and added, "Yes, she certainly looks a bit down," and thus my mother's illness seemed ratified.

After that Lucia began coming often again, but it was always—or it appeared to me—a visit to a sick friend, and at the door she never said, "Walk me home." Even if we saw each other at concerts, we were no longer the friends we had been at the liceo. When we met outside, she didn't ask about my mother: as if it were of no importance, or as if she trusted only her own eyes. Or as if it were a real, grave disease, I said to myself. It haunted me: Then she is ill, I thought. My mind raced to her death, to her, lying with her white hair under the light of the lamp, and to my life without her, a life which, in my still detached and basically incredulous imagination, was a problem of maids: how to hire one, for what hours, how to keep an eye on her, how to manage her in my own inability to manage. And if she steals, what must I do? And I thought of Lucia, then, who would help me. That was all.

I WAS IN my last year at the university and was preparing my thesis. At the bursar's office, which no longer seemed such a beautiful place to me, I met Diego one day.

He came toward me and narrowed his eyes, as if he were nearsighted, then bent over and took my hands affectionately.

"Marzietta, it's you. I hardly recognized you. It's been ages. You've grown up. And you've turned into a pretty girl, too!"

I asked him what he was doing.

"Nothing special. And you?"

"Chemistry."

"My God, you're really brave, Marzietta! Oh, I'm enrolled here, too, but not very seriously, in economics. . . . Yes, I'm economizing in economics, you might say; I take an exam every year or two. . . . But tell me about yourself. And your mother?"

I told him, vaguely. I was really pleased by this meeting, with no embarrassment, with the old intimacy of childhood, which seemed to have remained intact even if we hadn't seen each other for years and I had never thought of him again. I told him sincerely that I had almost forgotten him.

she were really amused at having a blood sample taken.

"Don't get in the habit, though," she said as he left. A moment later she was no longer in a mood to joke, and the solitude with me was heavy all the rest of the morning.

I thought again of those words of hers, echoing my secret concern that she was really ill. "You sleep," she said to me when at night she felt bad. "You can't do anything for me anyway." I didn't sleep; I lay with my eyes staring toward the wall, and I started at her painful belches.

Lucia came often now and my mother dictated briefs to her. Lucia went back and forth between Ariccia and Via Marianna Dionigi, carrying papers, independent of my movements, so after a while I stopped offering to bring things for my mother from our house, but Lucia would ask me for one thing or another.

"Take this stuff back and bring me the De Cesare file. It ought to be in the bunch of papers to the right, can you find it?"

I went to the house and I stopped at the door of her room, looked at the old red damask on the bed and the pillow, and I thought of her white head there, with the lamp's halo; I heard in my memory the shake she gave the book held in one hand to flip the page. A long painful sigh rose in me, within other images, not from my memory but as if they were already in it. How my mother would lie there dead, on that bed, Lucia moving about, knowing everything that had to be done; then in the silence of the house I heard the clock in the kitchen. And I ran to wind it, Elide's alarm clock, so it would never stop.

Or else I worked in the house, cleaning and straightening up, and so the solitude became a pleasure and I was happy, feeling the happiness, then, as guilt. If I had some-

"Well, I didn't really . . . Well, maybe I had forgotten you, too. I certainly didn't think I'd find you so changed. My God, you're really quite a girl now."

I laughed. I told him he was the first to say this to me.

"And you're a liar, too. Good. That's the way. Now your old friend Diego's going to buy you some ice cream. You want one, don't you? Come on, a girl should never refuse an ice cream."

"How is . . . h-how is your m-mother?"

"Mammina? Oh she's all right. An ache and a pain here and there, but not bad. I'm crazy about her, my mammina . . ."

We said good-bye at the tram. I remembered his mother well, old to be his mother, and a whiner, a kind of friend of my grandmother's whom my grandmother helped somehow. She had a special smell, and she carried an ancient black leather handbag, which had turned almost green; it folded under the bar of the clasp, and she held it tight in her hand, by the leather, not trusting the handle. In it there was a very worn, colorless purse, which she opened with a shamed, jealous movement. The money she took from it—I had seen her do this a very few times, perhaps when I went with her to make some purchase—she then clutched in the palm of her hand, hiding it. I used to see Diego with her at my grandmother's house and we played together.

FAUSTO, FAUSTO, I shouted within me as I ran up the stairs, or I dreamed of him at bus stops or walking along the corridors of the chemistry building. But only at odd moments now. I studied a lot, and I was concerned for my mother.

She'll die, I thought, but peacefully, without anguish. She'll die, I thought, and mechanically I wondered whether it would happen in summer or winter, and what sort of black clothes I'd need. But it was a thought I didn't believe, because she was better: in fact, she seemed well again, and it was spring and everything smelled of flowers.

She didn't get up in the night any more. Only now the thermometer was always by her bed. I looked at it sometimes, and the mercury was low. Therefore, and because it was spring, I concluded she didn't use it, she had just forgotten it on the table.

Still I didn't dare remove it.

THE BEST HOURS were in the lab. I loved my scales; I was intoxicated by the elegant precision of my own movements, the sensitive touch of my fingers on the dials; I was thrilled by the little luminous screen and the race of the tenth of a milligram that, back and forth, closer and closer, finally came and rested on the indicator like a bird on its branch. I "sensed" the weight, the substance, whether it was powder or liquid; my hand seemed to evaluate its inner consistency, even its weight, through the little spatula or the pipette. It was spring. I was excited and I longed for Fausto, his piano, those tiny divisions of time that he kept in his fingers. I thought obscurely of the dominion of time, the instant of decision: the attack of the musician. The word said at *its* moment. All words said at their moments. And silence. The immense silences without anguish which also exist: the distant silence of the cockles in the sea's bed of ribbed sand at Santa Severa.

And if I murmured Fausto, Fausto, walking along the walls, I knew now that his name was only a bubble surfacing in the flowering desert of my youth, content with itself.

IN THE EVENING I studied and then I went to look at my mother, from the doorway, barefoot so I wouldn't be heard; and I looked at her hair on the pillow and her hand, fleshless now, clasping the book. She coughed, at times, harshly, or forced a belch.—"There," she murmured at the end, alone, in her shaken bed, as when she laughed in company. I saw her again on the barge, down by the Tiber, with Viviana, and I felt now how pathetic those friendships were, to which she had given herself without reservation, with joy, with innocence. She will die, I thought. But perhaps it wasn't true that she would die. She was better. More than once, however, I had seen her remove the thermometer, look at it, shake it and put it back in its case with a trembling hand.

THE DAY I TOOK my degree the sirocco was stifling. I came home with top marks. My mother was moved; she had bought some pastries. I felt light and idle, already a bit bewildered. Still excited, I spoke very badly.

"Go rest a while, lie down, get some sleep. You must have slept badly last night. See what it feels like to rest on your laurels. Be careful they don't prick you, however. . . . So . . ."

She laughed. I felt tenderness for her, and sorrow, thin

as she was, the ropes of her neck taut; she covered them with her hands.

I went and flung myself on the bed, but my head was spinning and sleep wouldn't come. Half an hour later I got up, slipped on an old dress, my sandals, and went out quietly, without saying anything to her, in her study beyond the glass door.

I went down to the street by the Tiber. I walked for a long time, mute, and as if I were deaf as well. I formulated no words, I didn't speak. I went on, looking at my sandals, and my thought was a moan. The only real thing, and I felt it more and more, was the fear of meeting someone, anyone, and having to speak. That morning—so long ago—before the examining commission I had spoken all in a rush, almost always badly, but paying no attention. But now, no, I wouldn't have been able to speak. The fear that this could happen— meeting someone and having to speak—pressed within me like a ball of violence. I contained it and dragged it with me, all that long afternoon, through my streets.

Several times I passed below my home. Once, finally, because now the time of my walk had apparently consumed itself, I went into the entrance and climbed the steps. I remember that I felt the house above was empty, and I had my keys ready in my hand. But the door was open, and I had only to push the inner, glass door, and I don't know why I wasn't surprised by this. No one in the vestibule; no one in the study. Lucia appeared in the doorway of my mother's room, a finger to her lips. "She's running a high fever," she said. My eyes questioned her. "Thank goodness I was home when she telephoned," she answered. "When I got here she had vomited, but she had nothing in her stomach, she says. She was shaking, and, with this damn sirocco, she was cold as ice. She was shivering, and the whole bed shook, too. Where

69

the hell were you? I even called my house after you, when I was here. Thank God, I found my doctor, yours was out, or she hadn't called him, I don't know; anyway, mine came and he says he wants to see her again; for the moment, with this high fever, he can't say anything. It may be something simple that'll be gone tomorrow, but he asked me if she's had a temperature like this other times."

I thought of the times I had seen the thermometer on the table and in her hands. Meanwhile Lucia went toward the bed to take another look at her; she fixed the blankets and turned out the light on the table. "Now you can turn on the light in the hall," she said, and I was already obeying, under the fatal impression that it was to be done because she had said so and as if I had done the same thing other times, obeying her. She went to get her purse, which was in the bathroom. "Everything's in order here," I heard her say from in there. Alarmed, I asked if she was leaving. "Well, you can manage, can't you? She doesn't need anything now. Maybe some camomile when she wakes up. When Mazzetti comes back tomorrow morning, I'll come with him."

I realized Mazzetti was the doctor. Camomile? She will fix herself coffee as soon as she gets up, I thought to myself crossly. I didn't say it, but those words remained in my throat, preventing other ideas from taking shape and emerging. "She makes herself coffee," I grumbled to myself, when I should have said "So long" and "Thanks" to Lucia, who was leaving. "She makes herself coffee," I repeated inwardly when I was alone with my concern and remorse, looking from the doorway at her asleep. From the whole afternoon, the entire day, only those words remained with me. And still I was happy at heart for not having been there, happy she had called Lucia: also because of the clients who had surely been in the waiting room then, in the smoke of their cigarettes, until Lucia had sent them away. I was happy I hadn't had to send them away, and speak.

I went to see her during the night and I put my hand only near her forehead, for fear of waking her if I touched her. Her temperature was going down; two deep black hollows were forming under her eyes.

The next morning my mother was in her office and, when the doctor came later, he didn't find her because she had gone to court.

I WALKED A LOT those weeks after my degree, and I remember long sleepy mornings and afternoons. In the evening, and this was something new, my mother often didn't go straight to bed but went down with me to Ruschena's for an ice cream. Peppino and other friends were there. They talked, we laughed. The air was mild, the murmuring from the other tables around us was subdued. A suspended time, without expectation, which I enjoyed enormously. When we left, they walked us to our building, and there was only the stairway for the two of us to face alone.

One evening, while we were in the kitchen and it was still light and the children in the courtyard were still running and shouting in their summer games, my mother said, as she sliced the mozzarella: "I've been thinking—what do you say to this?—that I'm tired of working like a dog all the time; or rather, we're both tired, because you've worked hard, too, and we could go, the two of us, someplace for a while. Maybe nearby. Mazzetti thinks it would be a good idea. He says I have to turn off the engine a bit and recharge. He even wants me to give up coffee," she added, with a slightly forced laugh, "but that's too much. . . . So." She looked at me, seeking a smile of complicity. She was pathetic. I smiled.

"Well then, what do you say? Shall we go off, you and me? Cancel your engagements, and we'll have a bit . . . a bit of country air, I'd say. Nearby. You can go to the beach with your friends. I can't see myself at the shore, and by now you can't even find a closet anywhere near Rome, and I'm surely not the type for Riccione or Viareggio. We can take some things to read with us. . . . So."

Without stopping to think, I said, "What about kitty?" Maybe because we were at the table and at the table we always talked with the cat.

She shrugged—as was only right, I immediately thought, with remorse—and said, "The concierge will take care of him." And that was all she said.

Repenting that stupid objection, I tried to make amends, to ask more questions, to show interest. But it was late and she was already going to bed. I went to her room and she was reading by that time, the light on her hair. I was silent for a while, then I asked, with an effort, "Wh-when . . . do we l-leave?"

She shrugged her bare, white shoulders. "Who knows? If we *do* leave . . ."

I had begun to cling to the habit of the evening ice cream until it had become an obsession, a sharp desire that stayed with me all day, enriched with absurd prospects. And when we didn't go to Ruschena's then and I saw her go to bed, as I had seen her do for years, I was sharply disappointed. Reading and the radio, which had always been enough for me, were no consolation. I sat at the window on those evenings, with a lump of unhappiness and nastiness in my throat.

Finally, after a long time, one evening we went down

again for an ice cream. When we had been there half an hour, with Peppino and Carlo Briganti and his wife, Lucia appeared with a boy I didn't know. She was very smart, perfumed, aggressive. She left her man, who had friends at other tables, and sat with us for a while.

"Is everything arranged for Ariccia?" I heard her ask, as if it were an old matter.

"Will you go out there with me?" my mother asked. And she looked at Lucia's dress meanwhile, adding, "My, you're chic."

"Take you there? Of course, whenever you like. Even tomorrow, if you want. Peppino, what did you fix up, finally?"

She also used the *tu* in speaking to Peppino.

"I was waiting to hear from Sàlome. But she'll be delighted. I'll let you know in the morning. Sàlome still lives there."

"And are you going?" Lucia asked me. "Thank you," she said to the waiter.

"Wh-where?"

"To Ariccia, with Annetta," and she stared at her ice cream, not looking at me or my mother. My mother was talking about something else with Peppino, who called her Anna. Others, I remembered vividly at that moment, had called her Donna Anna: the friends from the time when she was young and we went to Ostia. It had seemed false and affected to me then; like certain expressions. "Especially," for example. With that extra "e."

Lucia went on eating her ice, in silence.

So we were going to Ariccia, without having talked again of going away. I didn't think she could possibly want to go alone. It was all settled by now, Lucia and Peppino had dealt with everything, and some woman with a Biblical name; I had done nothing, known nothing. But I would go,

I would be with her. I no longer enjoyed my perfumed evening on the Tiber; I felt anguish at the unknown departure, the prospect of long silences with her.

YOU DIDN'T ENTER through the front gate, which was always shut. You went through a little shop, fashions and notions, run by the gray Sàlome, and you came out into the sloping, shady garden. In the shade, the ground was still green with a wintry velvet. Farther on, unfenced, the chickens pranced around. The dog chewed an inexhaustible bone. Et cetera. I faced the big garden and the houses that lived in it, distrustful, happy only that Rome was near and the buses were frequent. I put up with sugary formalities from Sàlome, from her husband, from her ancient mother. My mother smiled, her teeth enormous in her sallow face; Lucia darted here and there, knowing everyone, greeted by all. Everything was false, in that hateful, false-bucolic vein. . . .

Then Lucia went off, that first evening, and as she said good-bye she touched my mother's forehead.

"Everything, I eat everything out here, in this country air," she said at the table, in the big room, which was cold even though it was July.

I looked at her with fear; I even spoke.

"Don't worry," she said to me, and looked at me, taking my wrist in her warm hand. "Don't worry, Marzia dear, don't worry."

I looked at her, into her long, painful smile—the two of us alone in the big room among strangers—and suddenly I broke down, moved by the truth of that smile of hers, by the gentle gesture of her hand on mine. And when we were

74

alone in the little house reserved for us at the other end of the garden, and she had sat down by the window to look through the darkness at the lights of Rome and the blue hills, I sat beside her.

Our elbows touched. We sat like that for a long time, without speaking. But it wasn't a heavy silence. I felt her hands near, not touching me, her white hair. Why are we here? I asked myself. Where is this? And we are together. But my old impatience began gnawing at me. I felt time flowing, I measured it. I have to unpack our suitcases, I was thinking; I have to unpack our suitcases. The words, aligned at first lightly behind the image, now took on body, became autonomous and strong. I have to unpack our suitcases. Words that became shouts. I had to say them; otherwise they would have hurt me, torn me. I have to unpack our suitcases. To break that precious silence, the night outside, and her hands, her hair near me: a shame. A few more moments, which I made as long as I could. But I had to say it.

I said, "I have to unpack our suitcases."

She sighed smoothly. There was still a tumult in my chest.

"Do it tomorrow," she said simply, serenely. "Who's rushing you?"

She was right. My anxiety slowly calmed down. She was right. I could go on sitting there. We sat for a long time, and I had no more minutes to measure within me.

The two beds were in the same room.

"What are you going to do? Read?" she asked me when we were under the covers.

"A little while. You read, too."

"No, I don't have anything."

"Your thriller . . ." I remembered, filled with guilt and dismay. I hadn't thought of it.

75

"No, no thriller. I'm bored with them, all those thrillers. All the same. Let's see if I can do without them. If anything, I'll read a brief, or the folders in the medicine boxes. Reading the folder is good for you, better than taking the medicine. Go ahead, read as long as you like."

I opened my book. But I wasn't at ease, with the light burning only for me and with her not reading. She spoke again, and, without turning, I imagined her with her hands clasped behind her head and her eyes looking at the ceiling.

"I wonder if there are scorpions here," she said. "When I was a little girl we used to go to Frascati. A house full of scorpions. The toilet was at the end of the balcony, suspended over the countryside. The cold that came up, from that hole . . ."

Sleep wouldn't come, even when I had turned off the light, because everything was so new. I didn't remember ever having slept in the same room with her. When I was little, I slept with Elide.

THERE WAS REAL BIRD SONG in the morning, in the distances of the countryside. We had smiles for each other. And I saw what warmth, in that different and perhaps truly richer human dimension, people so far from us in habit and thought could give.

She was tired, even more so in the morning. I saw her listen, her eyes greedy, to the stories of Sàlome, who folded little sweaters in her shop, and the stories of Sàlome's husband, who had a mustache. I saw her watching, for hours, the ancient Sora Medea, who talked to the hens.

Soon I, too, had lost the urgency of a thousand things,

as time stretched. I only missed my walks along the walls. The taste of the radishes reminded me of our courtyard and its smell.

She had another violent fever, with shivering and cold sweat, which left her exhausted. Soon she recovered, however, and was again in the garden and in Sàlome's shop. But she had deep shadows under her eyes and I saw them as we ate our hosts' cooking at the big table, noisy now with laughter, and I didn't know how far away—really how distant—were our little clear soups and mozzarellas on the white kitchen table, at home, under Elide's alarm clock.

Then I took the bus and went to Rome for an afternoon. At home I found the old shadows, the smell of her papers, the tired light of the study's glass door, and I felt everything as it had been before, insidious.

Colleagues of hers, friends for many years, came to Ariccia to see her; affectionate with her, I saw, as she was kindly and open with them. They talked about work, about lawsuits that had to be brought, but also of old matters that I didn't know or only partly remembered; and I was sadly surprised, again, by that whole texture, that warmth of affections she drew after her, up there, or that up there was being revealed to my remorse. And at evening, with my arms cold on the stone of the windowsill while I filled my eyes with the black countryside's immense sky and the winking lights of Rome, while I called, Fausto, Fausto, to rouse myself, I felt the room behind me brimming over with her first sleep and I understood that her life had been fuller and more worthy, more true and good than mine had been.

Lucia came, and to me it seemed she walked on our day as if on water, finding everything natural, chattering here and there, laughing, taking her by the arm along the rocky path. They paid no attention to it, they went down as if it were nothing, as if it had always been like that, and as if they had always had rocks and hens underfoot. This was perhaps jealousy in me.

But then, as Lucia was leaving, beyond the door of the little shop, she took my hand and wouldn't let go, and said, "Yes, she's better, she's more rested, but I'm not so reassured; she seems vague, almost asleep. I don't know. And her eyes are yellow. So long now. Keep in touch."

She went off in her little Fiat 600, which was new but already assimilated; she had stopped talking about it, as she ignored every other novelty after a while. I thought I had been unfair and Lucia had observed and understood my mother in those few hours better than I had in a month, and again I was pleased and grateful that she worried about us, and I was grateful now for the hens and the chatter of Sora Medea and Sàlome's husband. I went down the rocky path and I thought that when my mother was back in Rome, in her usual life, she would still keep this new softness, these humble interests, and her smile and pleasure at looking at the night sky or walking among stones. But I thought too that this return to primitive innocence—which I still felt incongruous with her nature—must be a preparation for death. And, I haven't much time, I haven't much time, I would say to myself, running for the bus that would take me to Ariccia when I was in Rome, and I felt that our meeting again after barely an afternoon's separation would mean for me and for her the rediscovery of a tender relationship which I didn't remember but now demanded of my imagination as my due.

I met Diego again.

"What? Don't you say hello to old friends any more? You're running like a bullet. Hi."

"Diego! I hadn't seen you."

"Come on. Your old friend Diego'll keep you company. Where are you going?"

"To catch my bus. I'm going to Ariccia."

"At this time of the afternoon? You're going dancing, I bet."

"Oh, naturally! I'm staying up there. With . . . Mamma. On a vacation, you might say. . . ."

"In Ariccia, of all places."

"What do you mean?"

"Oh, nothing. Is your mamma well?"

I answered without speaking, without saying anything.

"What time does your bus leave? If your old Diego had a car, he'd drive you. And maybe even take you dancing."

"I don't know how to dance. Here's the bus. So long, I've got to run." I caught the bus and remained standing, looking at the street lights that fled past. I felt a sorrow which didn't abandon me until night.

"Did you see Lucia in town?" my mother asked. I found her in the square, standing, chatting. Immediately, she seemed different from how I had remembered and imagined her in the apprehension of my trip.

"You didn't see her? I sent her to the house to look up some papers for me. She'll be coming tomorrow."

"I could have brought them to you. If you had phoned me . . ."

She didn't answer. Shrugging, she started chatting with the others again.

She had another bad spell. Days with a high fever, which didn't come down even in the morning. Mazzetti arrived, said he would send someone to take a sample of her blood for tests. He told me he couldn't say anything until he had seen the results of the tests.

When the man came, my mother joked with him, as if

thing to do in the study, I entered almost on tiptoe. The big lampshade, the silent desk with heaps of files and the blotter; in the silence they became gigantic again, as they had been when I was a few years old and was forbidden to go in there.

I DREAMED OF DIEGO'S MOTHER, whom I hadn't seen for so many years. She was on the tram, the Circolare Rossa, on the long wooden bench beside me. This was the tram of our departures for Ostia in my childhood, the trip to the Pyramid; and in my dream, too, we went to the Pyramid; then we got off and there was only an empty kennel or something like it; but the woman who was with me was afraid a dog was in there and she led me in a long detour through little gardens, all withered. And then we climbed toilsome stairs and she had become Maria the dressmaker, who dragged me by the hand, and her index finger was all rough because of the needle's scratches, and she said, "Quiet, sweetie, quiet, sweetie," and a little canary trilled violently in the air. "A little kiss, a kiss," Maria the dressmaker said and she gave me the little kiss, but she was again Diego's mamma, who now made me feel sorry and pitying, an immense tenderness in which I woke, full of enigmas.

WE HAD BEEN UP THERE for weeks; for months she had been ill. And I haven't done anything, I said to myself suddenly. I haven't even spoken to Mazzetti. Mazzetti had come and had talked with her. I had learned from her that the tests hadn't shown anything, only a slight deficiency of red corpuscles; but I hadn't seen the results of the analysis.

I haven't done anything. It struck me, like that, for the first time; but I also knew it wasn't true that I hadn't thought of it before, and I was lying to myself to hide my fear and guilt. I had to do something, move, speak to Mazzetti, take her to another doctor.

But she wouldn't let another doctor examine her.

"My digestion's bad. Millions of people have bad digestion," she would say. I would discuss it with Lucia.

Lucia told me to meet her in Piazza Cavour. Because she had things to do in the neighborhood, she said. I was as nervous as if this were some clandestine rendezvous. Lucia was lively, more bubbling than usual. We went along Via Ulpiano, but she didn't have her usual briefcase full of papers. I was surprised, because she had told me she had business around there.

Finally I interrupted her flow of chatter. I said I didn't like the way my mother was, Mazzetti hadn't told me anything. . . . She didn't answer right away.

"Mazzetti hasn't told you anything, you say? Anything about what?"

"I don't know," I said. "Those blood tests, for example. I wanted to go and collect the results, but he picked them up himself. I never got a look at that analysis."

"Did Annetta see it?"

"I don't know. She says she did."

"In other words, you're worried." Her tone, her pace changed, and it wasn't necessary for me to answer.

"You're worried." She walked slowly now, looking at the ground. We went on like that for a long time, but I knew she was always thinking the same thing and she knew I was waiting.

Then she said: "One day you were home, or at the university; here in Rome, I mean. I went out there and Mazzetti came and the two of us left together. I didn't have my car so he drove me back into town. He told me I was right, Annetta is not well. She's very ill, in fact. He told me that he admires her, and I agreed with him. But that isn't the point, either. To make a long story short: when he appeared, the case had already been diagnosed. She diagnosed it by herself. By herself, you understand?"

Her voice had changed. Or it was my senses; the slabs of the sidewalk for a moment had come close to my eyes. I let her talk. I was surely in no hurry.

She said: "You remember when she began having a fever, running a little temperature; you wouldn't even know how often, because you don't touch her. Well, she diagnosed it herself. She found some growths under her armpits, like little balls; and then she went to somebody or other, she studied the medical encyclopedia, and she had her blood tested. All on her own. It was amazing, Mazzetti said, because it was a difficult diagnosis, a rare disease, a thing you and I have never heard of. Not me, anyway. Hard even for a doctor to figure out, and she did it alone. Maybe she knew somebody who had had it," she added softly," and that's why she didn't want you to call a doctor. It isn't a tumor, but it's like one in many ways. It's a disease of the lymphatic glands, it's called lymphogranuloma. It's also called malignant granuloma. I think . . . You must have understood. She's an extraordinary woman," she went on in a louder voice, "a good woman. Now she'll start taking a medicine that will make her feel better, but she can't get well. That's how it is, you understand: she controls the situation, and Mazzetti obeys her. She doesn't want you to know. As long as it's possible, she said. She says she knows and that's enough; she says she can do what she wants, because that's the advantage of an incurable disease when you know you have it."

Finally I stopped, because I wanted to, and I forced her to look at me. She read the question in my eyes.

"Maybe several years," she said. "It can change form, attack various organs, or it can remain generalized. Something can be done against it. Radium. The funny thing, the funny thing is . . ." and here Lucia gave a little, grotesque laugh ". . . is that Mazzetti tried to tell her she had made a mistake, had made the wrong diagnosis, that she might be a great lawyer but as a doctor she was all thumbs. . . ."

She hid her face in her hands for a moment. Then she started to run. We were at the end of the façade of the Palazzo di Giustizia toward Sant'Angelo, at the little lawn with the cats. She ran off like that, along the curve of the garden, leaving me alone. My first impulse was to run, too, but my legs failed me, and I slowed to a heavy walk. I overtook her finally, with dry eyes, stiff. Because I had known it, I explained to myself mechanically, I repeated to myself. I had known everything already, before she told me. But she was crying. Her hair was dirty, in sticky, awkward clumps at the nape of her neck. I put my hand under her arm and she almost fell on me, crying. I didn't cry. I felt her emotion jar on me, strike me, as the rustication of the palazzo jarred on my sight.

Then we walked on and she immediately stopped sobbing. She didn't talk any more. I felt a violence ready within me if she had. We walked at the same, hard pace. Again in the square, we walked around the gardens, but on the outside, on the pavement, not as in the days when we studied together and crossed the paths. I could hear again the crunch of the gravel as I had always heard it, from Elide's time, and I thought that now I couldn't, now the days of gravel were over. Then I thought this notion was histrionic, and it irritated me.

Our footsteps on the sidewalk made too much noise, there was too much noise around us; her presence beside me was intolerable, it disturbed my silence, disturbed everything. I wanted to get rid of her then and there. But I thrust her toward her house. And suddenly I felt her beside me as if she were smaller, weaker. We stopped, without having slowed down.

I said, "You said I never touch her."

My voice was hard, my eyes on the ground. Then I raised them to hers; between them there was a deep furrow. She held my gaze a long time, and I admired her for this. Then she turned and left me, running toward the door. Then the thing burst in me and I ran. I ran to the Palazzo di Giustizia, and then the length of Piazza Cavour, with the scream inside me.

IN THE BUS I managed to sit down and I looked at the houses, the countryside, the great curves of the road. I was imagining a grave, how small it is: how little space she would take up, underground. And all her books. So many and so heavy on their shelves. All her papers covered with her round, squat writing, a man's hand. I saw the interpolations in those lines, superimpositions in Lucia's writing: a cheap device, worthy of the movies.

I realized I was crying. But the tears were still this side of my guilt or remorse; my sorrow. It was a weeping this side of everything, as yet.

I stepped into the square when it was night, and the

85

song of the fountain, eternal there, replaced the rhythm of the bus. I was alone, and: It's not true! I shouted within myself. It wasn't true, what Lucia had said. For a long time, for months, I had known that my mother would die, and now I couldn't accept it from Lucia, who had dared tell me that other truth: ". . . You don't touch her."

The shop was closed by now and they had left the creaking gate open for me. The big trees were silent. I tried to muffle my footsteps as I went down the steps and over the stones to our little house, which was alight. I imagined her in bed; but she wasn't there. She must be at Sàlome's house already. She had left the light on for me. I thought that for a long time: She's left the light on for me. I stubbed my toe against the foot of the bed. The pain was sharp and I sank on the bed, clutching my foot. I started crying. I cried, rocking with pain, anger and self-pity. Then, in that weeping, I found my way to those other tears.

IN THOSE FIRST DAYS, when to look at my mother was to spy on her and to think, She knows, I ran into Diego. He rushed up to me and grabbed my arm.

"I jumped off the tram to see you. How's everything? Your mamma?" he asked, with eyes immediately severe, from which I drew back. "Still in the country? One of these days I'll come and see her, if she still remembers me. Tell her."

He must have read it in my face: that I wouldn't have known how to tell her, about this child of my grandmother's friend whom she may or may not have remembered.

"You don't want me to? A nuisance for you? Forget it

then. How do you like it up there? Good wine and fresh eggs, eh?"

I was grateful to him and I hastily started saying, Yes, yes, fresh eggs—from Sora Medea—but maybe her name was Amedea—and how a few days before she had fallen down the steps of the henhouse and hadn't hurt herself at all. Ninety years old.

"Ninety! Go on, she lies about her age. Like my mammina. She's sixty-two, but to hear her . . ."

And he went on, in his fluent way. Then we each had some ice cream, which he paid for. I was touched, as if by a huge, undeserved present. I watched him eat his: with greed and attention, like a child. And I asked him, "What are you doing?" to make him talk some more, for no other reason.

"I'm licking my ice cream," he answered, almost with a start. I laughed.

"No, I mean, with your life."

"Oh, life! Life is big. There are lots of things to do. Today, for example, I ran into a pretty girl and I'm taking her for a walk."

WE WERE STILL at Ariccia and Diego made dates with me. He talked about everything; I didn't tell him about my mother. And when I thought of her, while he and I were together in the streets, I forgot him. And then her nearness, her profile, her hand on my arm, her words: I felt them, suddenly, beyond an abyss.

I LOOKED AT HER. I listened to her breathing at night, when her awareness was asleep. I watched her face in the night's shadow, on the white bed, and I imagined that at least dreams for her could still be without death. Dreams like those before, like everyone's. The same as in childhood. Her childhood: incredible until then for me, beyond imagining. Alive and tangible in her talk about it now.

I saw her, if I woke up, in the armchair with a book. She had got up because of her impatience, her intolerance of the bed which came over her now almost every night, around two A.M. But then she was serene, wrapped in the blanket, the book in her hands, bending over it a bit; not out of weariness of her position, it seemed, or weakness, but because she was intent on her reading. She followed the lines with her eyes wide, a relaxed but alert expression, of great tranquillity. At times she made a little noise with her mouth, clucking behind her teeth, to one side. It was the little tic of an old woman, and my grandmother had made it, too, exactly like her.

And yet, beneath her diligent, calm attention, the book was always the same. And what a book. Sàlome had given it to her, a book she would never have read, one that I would never have allowed myself to be caught with, either. She read like that, an hour, two, even three hours. And she didn't sleep. I did, for long stretches; and then I woke up, because the big light had been turned on, and again I would watch her.

Along the rocky path, which I thought it strange my mother could cover so well—not only because of her present suffering, but because of the contrast with the habit of a life-time, which had been almost a religion of city streets—I found my mother with Peppino one day. I went toward them as they climbed up—and despite the short distance, they seemed small to me, in a remote perspective. I saw many things of their past, when they had often been together and very close once and now no more, and I also remembered her words: "And his girl friend is next door. Life comes to funny conclusions, but I don't give a damn." I watched them approach, savoring the sight of their slow steps as if it were a very long performance: also, to delay the moment of meeting and speaking. They said, "Here's the daughter. Now we'll sit in the shade and talk."

I was afraid they wanted to talk with me about the disease and it seemed almost trivial when, instead, they told me they had found a way for me to enter the Lavoisier Institute. Incredulous, I said it was very difficult, impossible to get in there. But I said it still as if this were a game, relieved they hadn't talked of that other thing. And they said, you're silly, that naturally one had to know something, and then—what did it matter?—with a degree as brilliant as yours, you can achieve that and more, and don't forget: Dress well, fix your hair, talk freely and don't be shy; that would be all wrong.

When Peppino had gone, the smile died on my mother's suffering face, and she took my arm and leaned hard on me as we went back toward our little house. The silence between us was heavy, and while I told myself that I should speak, she said briefly, "You're as good as the others, don't forget that."

In the house, she lay down for a while on the bed, before supper time. I offered to bring some supper to her there.

"No, I'll come with you," she said. "We mustn't disappoint people waiting for us."

By now every sentence of hers was engraved in me, pregnant with meanings.

Later, when her breathing had become that of sleep, I sat at the window. Now I thought of my new job, my first job. I felt only a little nostalgia for the scales in the old chemistry building. Meanwhile, pride was already mounting in me. I imagined a new hair style for myself, a personage in that inaccessible place, totally perfect. The wind caught the tree below the window and shook it. Behind me, the door slammed. Starting at the noise, I thought with dismay: Now she'll wake up. But she didn't. I was alone with the darkness of the windy night over the immense countryside. With my new pride, my old angry defiance also rose in me. "I'll show them. I'll show them all." I didn't say, "I'll show them how I'll talk," because that was taboo; but that was what I was thinking. Always that. I'll show them. Them: Lucia, Diego and her, too. Yes, all of them. Her too, and I didn't think of her as she was at that moment, but as she had been for so many years, when she had had and said so many things. Said everything she had wanted to say, always.

IT WAS RAINING when we went back to Rome; it had been raining for several days. Lucia was there, and Peppino had gone, in his big, comfortable car, with no jolts for the sick woman who left that house and that garden, her eyes glistening, with good-byes from people who already loved her, who wept and laughed and promised to come very soon, of course, and maybe bring her a wine flask full of the water from the fountain in the square, that fresh water better than medicine.

Lucia had been at home with me to prepare everything,

90

mostly the bedroom, because the papers in the study were already in order; she herself, in those months, had checked all the movements back and forth to Ariccia and had gone frequently to the courthouse for my mother. The bedroom was now really a sick room, with a white napkin on the dresser for medicines and a hot plate to boil the syringe. Lucia moved about the house with confidence, precision: more efficient than I was. When she had left—and I had anxiously waited for her to go—I went back to my mother's room with the intention of changing many things, but then I changed nothing.

So the next day my mother came, accompanied by Peppino, who parked the car right in front of the door of the building. Because of the little stone post, he couldn't come into the courtyard; otherwise he would have, he said, and this concern to spare her those few steps seemed false and affected to me, exaggerated after all the walking over stony paths that she had done. But then I noticed the sad, frightened face of the concierge, who was seeing her after a two months' absence; I observed the effort it cost her to climb the three steps to the elevator, the big livid shadows on her face, the forced smile; I saw her come into the house and sit down at once. Absurdly I wanted to say, Let's go back to Ariccia.

She went to bed and said that maybe she had a bit of fever and she wanted to take her temperature, like that, in front of everyone. At that moment, I realized, she was admitting she was ill. We were left alone. I fixed something for her in the kitchen. We hardly ever spoke. Only: "Are you tired?" I asked her, and it was foolish, but she answered politely, "A little."

Then she said, "Turn out the light, but stay here," and I turned out the light and stayed beside her in a great silence. The period of Ariccia was over and would never come back.

I had never had such a feeling of an end. I took her hand, which was cold, and warmed it in mine.

DIEGO CALLED ME and I went out with him. Short walks, because I never went far from the house for long. Diego talked and talked and I liked listening to him; tenderly he took my arm, and I felt a tenderness toward him. He talked, told me stories, and I was withdrawn, suddenly struck by the thought that in all these months I hadn't told him. "She's ill? Since when? What? You didn't tell me?" I could almost hear him. And while he talked—fond, affectionate, but what did he talk about?—I covered his real words with those others, imagined, of reproach, and so I began to feel an irritation toward him.

We went by Via Pietro Cavallini, and outside the door of what had been my grandmother's building—but the curtains at the windows above were different—between the two little walls of the flowering hedges, he kissed me and he said, "Marzietta, Marzietta" . . . and then, "You aren't really fond of me. You aren't fond of me enough."

Afterward, afterward, I screamed inside me, as I thought of the dark stairway of the house, the house deserted except for her who shook the bed with the shivers of her fever, and then, "I must go, let me go," I said, and I ran off.

I ran up the steps then, with remorse for him left behind down at the door, and, when I got there, I sometimes found her calm, or else I found her really in need of me, but all the same I shut myself in the bathroom, and, with my face buried in the bathrobe hanging from its peg, I would shout, "Diego, Diego, forgive me, forgive me for leaving you like that, I didn't want to leave you and I didn't even tell you, I told you nothing, nothing; I've never told you anything."

But the great sorrow in me would not be released, my remorse at not having yet told him she was so ill. I thought of him walking along the street, his footsteps again in front of the same shops as a moment ago when we were together; and I was up there alone. Finally I went to her, I made her eat—the little she ate—and settled her for the night, and, when she was asleep, I sat at the window and would have liked to talk to him who wasn't there, like that, against the wall of the courtyard, but even solitary words wouldn't come, or I could barely moan, "Afterward, afterward": a promise without hope.

At night my mother hardly slept, now, except for the first hours, and she couldn't tolerate her bed. Then in the morning she dozed off, to wake late, after ten, when the doctor came for the intravenous injections and the vitamin shots. She took Chloramine orally and the days when she had taken it secretly were in the past. It was now tacitly understood between us that I knew; the accord had developed imperceptibly and she had accepted it simply. She got up with an effort, but except for the days when her temperature was high, she wanted to, because, "If I stay in bed one day, then I won't get up again," she would say; and she went to the study, where sometimes there was a client, or only Lucia, who helped her. The glass door was no longer shut and I often saw her at her big desk, motionless, livid shadows under her closed eyes, her hands lying limply on her papers. But if I approached, to pull her shawl around her—yes, now she wore that old shawl that had been my grandmother's—or smooth her hair with my fingers, I felt defiantly Lucia's presence even if Lucia wasn't there. And I smiled happily at my mother— the happiness of those moments!—if she raised her enormous eyes to me, but without moving her hands from that limp position which inspired respect and tender shyness.

I don't remember everything of that period: the various cures that were tried; the radium applications that exhausted her; then the sudden, always briefer periods of improvement. And Diego, always Diego in the streets, along the black, wet, gleaming sidewalks of autumn, Diego in my silent tenderness, in my remorse at my silence. I remember Lucia, as I used to see her: alert, efficient, good, cruel. Yes, words: I chose them carefully and applied them to her, watching her. Indispensable Lucia. I sat idle at the foot of my mother's bed with some knitting in my hands, and I heard Lucia in the study, typing, shuffling papers, speaking with the clients. Her eyes closed, my mother was immobile, white. This is how she would be, I thought. She never spoke to me of Lucia, except to have me call her.

"Get her in here a moment," she said. In the way she said "her," I felt a delicacy in not naming Lucia too often in front of me. She came and they discussed their work while I was half absent. I didn't follow their discussions, but I listened to their voices, observed their faces. Like a dog, I thought. And then I watched Lucia go out of the room and she seemed to grow bigger as she went away; I thought of her then, seated always in my mother's chair at the desk, through the years of the future. Her face, her movements, more mature, then old, always behind that desk, and smoke and people in the room with the glass door, while my mother would be the same as she was now, white, her eyes closed.

I still hadn't told Diego. Until one evening, when in the street I said, "I have to go back, I have to go home," he held on to me.

"What's wrong with you? Why do you always have to run off like Cinderella? Tell me what's wrong; why don't you tell me, eh?" He held me by the wrist, and with his other hand he caught me by the nape. I felt the warmth of his hand in my hair. "Tell me once and for all, and you'll feel better, I know there's something wrong that you aren't telling me. Tell me. Out with it. Or do you want me to tell you? Is that it? Shall I tell you?

"Come," he said again, making me turn. And he really did tell me. "It's your mother, and she's ill, isn't that it? That's what it is, isn't it? I know it. I figured some of it out for myself, and the rest your friend told me, Lucia. Come on," he said again. "Come here, stay a little while with me this evening, just a little longer."

Finally it was enough. I fell against him, my face against his chest, and burst into tears. He stroked my hair and remained silent. Until I spoke. I don't know how badly I spoke, but like a stream suddenly freed, I told him at last about how ill she was and how she would die, even if he already knew it. "And I," I said, "I'm silly, and wicked, and I don't deserve anything because you're good and you stay with me and keep me company, and I tell you nothing, you see, I never told you anything, ever, you see, and it's the same with her, I've never told her anything, not even that I loved her, and I've never kept her company, never. . . . No, no, it's true, because with the fact that I can't talk, no, no, that isn't it, not all of it, but that too, and so many things. . . ."

He stopped stroking my hair. He took my hands and slowly raised them to his face and kissed them, together. "Stop it," he said softly. "Stop it now, come here, and don't talk any more nonsense."

"Really, really, I mean it." I sobbed.

"All right, have it your way, you don't tell me things: maybe because you don't want to tell me them. Okay, have it your way; all right, yes, yes, whatever you say, we know you aren't a great talker . . . what of it? You think your Diego doesn't know that? You think he doesn't understand? You're the one who mustn't forget that Diego loves you, and, if you do, you really are wicked; and besides, when it comes to talking, I'd say one chatterer is enough in the family; by God, that's why I never achieve anything worthwhile; but you, without a word, look at all the things you've done. I mean it; when I think about it myself, sometimes it doesn't seem possible that a girl like you would come out walking with me, damnit. And you say these things to me. You talk, you don't talk . . . what's the difference? Come on now, be good, stay a little longer with me, just a minute, and then you can go home to your mamma, poor thing. You go to her and tomorrow you'll come back to me for a little, all right? All right? Her and me, and that's all, isn't it? And you know what I say: When it comes to the others, all the others, don't let them bother you!"

I didn't cry any more, or talk. A great silence, a peace, had descended on me, which received one by one his precious words. And yet, later, at the window on the courtyard, while my mother slept and her breathing filled the night, I thought again of how he had already known what I had wanted to tell him for such a long time, just as she had always already known the things that, with effort, I had always told her too late. And I knew that, still, the tumult in me was not spent.

THOSE WERE ALSO the first weeks of my job. In the morning I went out early, happy in the gray air, full of resonance. Happy to board every day the same bus, proud of my role as a working woman. A personage: like the flower woman at the corner, the morning milkman in American films, the school-master, the grandmother: ordinary, conventional, beloved by all. In those moments I adored mankind and in my spirit I sacrificed to it, paying for my ticket, half-price at that hour, dreaming of somehow possessing mankind in this way. As I then walked past the morning's cold wall, I recited my old poems, I sang my old music, and, since in them I found the sweet, ancient tears, I sought them every day, until poems and music lost their flavor and their power.

Then the immense reflecting corridors of the institute, the perfect laboratory, swallowed me up: the personage. And yet here too the bottles in the closets had labels stained by drops of reagents. The directress of our section, for the sake of economy, they said, didn't go to the refectory "or home, to doze in bed for a bit like a human being," but at two o'clock cooked an egg over the Bunsen burner and then fell asleep at her desk, her head on her folded arms. The secretary suffered from monthly afflictions so painful that she had to spend at least a day away, resting, and the terrible directress kept a calendar on the girl and began to grumble a few days ahead of time: "Naturally on Wednesday Miss De Carolis will stay home with her stomachache." But while in this way the unattainable temple of science took on dimensions even laughably human, my personage, day after day, tried desperately to keep itself intact. I didn't want to see that role fade, because it contained my hopes of learning how to talk one day, perhaps even soon, like everybody else.

Eight, ten hours away from home. The thought of my mother in those hours was tender, good. With her, I hardly stammered at all any more.

WHEN I REACHED HOME, I went at once to my mother and smiled at her. I smiled at her all the time now.

"Guess who paid me a visit?" she said, in a pitifully sly manner, which alarmed me. "Elena Brosio, no less. You remember her? How long ago it was! She's still the same, with her hair dyed and her whining chatter. Poor thing, she kept me company," she concluded in a fading voice, as she turned toward the wall. "Would you turn out the light?" she said.

I turned it out and left the room, filled with sudden rebellion. Elena Brosio was Diego's mother. Now it seemed to me the old, unpleasant odor of that woman lingered in the whole house. Why had she come? Diego had sent her. Resentment toward him sprang up, became enormous in an instant, stubborn and nasty. Who asked him to send her? "Who asked him to send her?" I repeated angrily, while I took off my coat and, with brusque movements, hung it in the closet. "Who told him to send her here and what does she want, what does she want?"

It wasn't until late that evening that I saw Elena Brosio as she had been in my mother's gentle words. "Poor thing, she kept me company." As if to say that, now, even Elena Brosio was company for her. "How long ago it was," she had said. In those days there was my grandmother, the mother from whom she had broken away, torn herself free, without pity. For me those days had been the apartment in Via Pietro Cavallini, Elide speaking softly in a corner with my grandmother, Maria the dressmaker who sewed my little dresses: all the old things I thought I regretted and now I realized I was glad were dead.

Elena Brosio continued to visit my mother and soon I

98

learned to be grateful to her for it. Coming home, at times, I found them still together. I had feared my mother would be irritated by those visits, that chatter: gossip about people long dead; instead I saw she was happy, brightened, and in joking at my expense she became Elena's accomplice as she had once been Lucia's. A little drawing room almost every evening at the foot of her bed.

But when I met Diego I didn't speak to him about his mother's visits; I allowed this new silence to grow between us, more swollen every day.

AN INFECTION suddenly caused my mother two weeks of delirium. She didn't suffer and remained awake, even calm, but her mind wandered among old memories that became present ones and the impression that she was on a journey. "When are we going to arrive?" she would ask. "This journey's too long; it's stupid. The country is so beautiful and they don't even let me look out of the window." Then she wanted to get up. She slipped on her robe, and with the expression and punctilious movements of an obedient child she buttoned every button and tied the belt in a knot. "There," she said. "Now we'll go and see the sprout. Are you coming too?" And she smiled at me. I smiled at her, while my sorrow was placated at the sight of her serenity. She wanted to walk, and she thought she was somewhere else, in a foreign country, and then: "It's not wrong at all," she said, "but it's a shame."

I was silent with myself, waiting. Waiting for her to be as she was before, or grow worse, or die. Hour by hour, I felt this time was temporary, a vacation granted her from suffering; to me, waiting. Her mind wandered; it was as if she weren't there. And yet a dizzying truth pressed on the unreality of those hours. "We'll go and see the sprout? Are you coming too?" A smile of hers, a smile of mine; a bit of opera, our little "mad scene." It was true. Her mind, she herself, was like this now; was this. But the sprout was real: even if I didn't know what it was, because certainly the word meant another word. And I stayed there making thoughts and mounting them on words. I could allow myself this; I could, but not she! This was how I had stayed by the bed of Elide, grumbling thoughts that were complete, desperately formed from dead words.

Lucia came in and talked with her, made her answer or talked about her as if she weren't present. Elena came and couldn't enter the room; she stayed in the door, her hand on her mouth, her eyes immense, black.

Then the fever dropped and the delirium abruptly ended. She was again as she had been before, but she suffered worse than before. The blood transfusions were intensified. It went on another month; she was perfectly herself, talking.

That month I looked at her all the time. She was very thin. Only her arms possessed a frightful strength. She took the glass from my hand furiously, with joy—her only joy now—and she drank. One evening, spectral as she was, while she drank the water she said, "Chaste, pure . . . Saint Francis was right."

SHE WAS THERE, dead, and, in my mind, I postponed. Afterward, I said, afterward I'll be able to think about it. I walked around the house, I stopped at the windows. Lucia and Elena were present. Had been always, from some profound time. I had looked at them, I had seen them always, lucidly. I knew all their movements, their strange way of agreeing, different as they were, their words, their going out in turn so as not to leave me alone. I looked at them and I laughed inwardly, because I knew everything about them and it didn't interest me. The obstacle was something else. It was that body on the bed, the obstacle between me and the true memory of her. Afterward, afterward.

That night, after the body had given its last jerks and had fallen back so that everyone had said my mother was dead, they made me stretch out on my bed. I knew that the concierge and her husband were in her room; I knew why, and I didn't care. I, I had nothing more to do; nothing more, ever: because everything I had done since birth had been because she had asked me to. Now I was poor like everyone else who didn't have her. And so I fell asleep.

Wakefulness seized me early because of the cold in the room, unnatural in the dawn that entered through the open window, and I was gripped immediately by the guilt of sleep's oblivion. I ran and found only the cold silence and the repulsive smell of flowers around the cold thing that was not my mother, not even the suffering body that had belonged to me. That taut smile, ironic and forced, and the high forehead with the airy white hair: they had made it "theirs," it was something of theirs and I didn't want to remember them. I went to look at the day in the dull gray and yellow courtyard with the blind wall opposite, patterned only by the streaks of rain and by mold. Later, in the hall, I found Diego: an intruder.

"I'd stay," Lucia said to me that evening, "but Papa isn't well and Mama hardly ever sees me; do you mind if I go . . . or rather, come with me, come and sleep at my place, at least tonight."

I refused with private, triumphant sarcasm, certain of her relief, as I was of the words that she hadn't said: "For

101

tonight, then afterward you'll have to get used to it." When she had gone, I was left with that argumentative streak in me and, in the silent house, still full, it seemed, of the smell of flowers, with the reality that I wouldn't allow to overcome me, that I wanted to postpone and still had already accepted totally: her death. I felt that end, unmistakable and absolute. For she was not in the objects around me or even in my memories. These, if I tried to grasp them, drew back in a distance gilded with falsity. She was no more and the idea returned that if no one had her and I alone had possessed her, now, guilty and wretched but free, I was like everyone else. I could have talked now, I told myself, in the ticking of Elide's alarm clock, like Elena Brosio and Lucia and people in the movies, the women at the market, the hairdresser and all, all that mankind I sometimes worshiped, which talked, which made words even before existing, for me.

Lucia was about: mistress of her papers, of the study, of the bell and the telephone. To my feelings, my conscience, I would give other nourishment. Objects. The thrillers by the bed and her comb in the bathroom, or the robe that she had put on and taken off a thousand times in those months.

Elena had disappeared, in a discreet gesture. She had not spoken to me of Diego, never in those months, and, when they had met at my house, they had carried it off with naturalness.

THE FIRST TIME we saw each other alone after her death, Diego and I, he didn't speak. He took my arm and we walked for a long time. He let his steps be guided by mine, so I took him through my usual streets around there, to the Tiber, and up all the way to Ponte Rinascimento. I remember everything of that walk and his presence-absence beside me, the silence for which I was grateful to him. "I must really be a bore for you," I said finally, when we were again in front of my building.

And smiling he touched the tip of my nose with one finger and said, "Silly!"

I ran up the steps, filled with tenderness, love, emotion. That was the evening when I wrote him for the first time. I had no stationery and I went to take a pack of paper from the study. I can't talk to you because you don't have a telephone, I began, and already in the banality of that sentence and, even more, in the word "talk," there was a hidden sense of triumph. But I don't remember that first letter, and I haven't read it again. I know it was brief, made of little, emotional sentences. I folded the paper, I slipped it into a drawer and I went off to sleep. The pack of white paper remained on my desk.

THE DAYS WENT BY and I walked through the streets with Diego. He talked. He would end his little sentences with a "no?" or an "eh?" which expected no answer but were companionable, gave a meaning to my silent presence. Even when I did talk, afterward I felt as if I hadn't, and I remembered only him. He bent over me and pressed my arm, and said, "I'll go with you, to the door, to the bus, to the corner, to buy meat, eggs, to the hairdresser."

"But don't you have anything to do?" I would ask him, and he would say, "Of course, but it'll only take a minute. I'll go with you, eh? Or don't you want your old friend Diego along?"

I wanted him. Leaving him was always a painful wrench. And yet, more than before, when I was with him, I found my mind wandering. I walked, holding his arm, I looked at the ground, I followed our footsteps on the sidewalk, and my mind pursued other images and thoughts. I put together words and words then, as in the days of my solitary walks with the ghost of Fausto. Words, whole sentences, more and more complete. Then long stories with interjections, parentheses, one within the other, questions, answers, laughter. Dialogues between the two of us. But it was all inside me, all without my uttering a word really.

"Marzietta, what's wrong? Can't you hear me? Are you sleeping? You tell me something now."

I blushed and began talking then, wretchedly. Things different from those silently said, narrated, a moment before. Or I tried my best to repeat what I had imagined. Poor stuff. Forced words, not the tenth part of the long, happy talk I had had all inside me. A suffering, as of a dream between blind walls. And when he started talking again—to free me? tired of my efforts?—I emerged only little by little from the swamp that my talking had been.

Diego was kind. We went to the butcher's and he was the one who asked for the steak, the chop; he was tall and was looked at first, beyond the high counter, he who knew the cuts of meat, who talked so well, and also knew how to joke while he talked.

"Listen, your Diego's so hungry he can't see straight," he would say. "How about a couple of rice cakes? Come on. They make divine ones here." We ate the rice cakes, and I wanted to pay, because it wasn't right that he should pay all the time. "Forget it," he said, "you'll invite me to your house. . . . You know I'm a good cook. . . . Invite me, and then Diego will take over."

We walked along the walls. Embracing under the trees whose scent was heady. And then he carried my purchases to the house. "The bag's heavy for you, no?" And at the door, he would say a few words to me, the evening words, stroking my hair or touching me lightly under the chin. He never kissed me at the door, and I came up, alone, with the warmth of his tenderness.

I ate listening to the radio or reading. I looked at the cat and he opened his eyes a crack, letting out a little, soft sound. He was asking me to talk to him; then he would come and rub against my legs. Since my mother wasn't there any more, I was reluctant to talk to the cat. In the silent house I wondered if she was more dead for him than for me.

In the study, the cigarette smoke of Lucia and her clients remained; sometimes a light was burning, the typist was still at work. I didn't go in there any more.

I undressed and in my robe I rushed to write him. All day I had waited for that moment, even while I was with Diego, even with my eyes on his; I had waited for it all day, but only now I realized how intensely. I wrote greedily, my hand couldn't keep pace with the words. The words, my words, all that had been around me and in me that day and my whole life. Memories, desires, dreams, vague and precise images: finally they became words. I wrote to Diego as if he were facing me and I knew how to talk to him; but then I forgot Diego and went on writing, just writing, mildly enjoying the surprise of everything that rose in me and flowed onto the paper. Old things that, now, it seemed I had never known fully because I had never said them; in this way at last, they took on form, a form that belonged to me as nothing else, ever, had belonged to me. I wrote at length, happy, until my writing subsided and faded, slowly dying out, leaving me released and light. I thought no more about my love. I slipped the pages into the drawer, on top of all the others. I went to bed, I fell asleep after addressing a rapid thought to Diego in the darkness. Till tomorrow. I would see him tomorrow: the Diego who walked through the streets with me. Affectionate, dear, unknown.

SOON IT HAPPENED that, in his presence, I no longer dedicated long tales to him, happy even if mute. While I was with him I was silent, even within myself, only dreaming of the evening's silent solitude, and of writing. Serene, I listened to him talk.

And so my days settled into a welcome monotony. Solitude, work, walking with Diego and, at night, writing.

Often when I came out of the institute I went to the cemetery: visits that were soon full of peace. In them—and I knew it well—that image of my mother became fixed: the one that, piecing together one memory and another, mostly from the last months, I preferred to keep. I went to her grave and I greeted her; I addressed vague thoughts to her and even words which soon became always the same; and while thoughts and words were both for her, for the full, convenient memory of her that I was creating for myself, my imagination ran to the dead body that was there below, closed in zinc—and the scream of the flame that had soldered it returned—in zinc and wood, immured in the little space in the darkness. In the darkness was the subtle smile of her dead face. That false smile was present: precise in every detail more than any remembered expression of her alive. Elena returned, ambiguous, and Lucia, with her shameless truths: "Funny, yes, you were funny, both of you. You never said

106

anything to each other; she seemed to be afraid of you, she who wasn't afraid of anybody; both of you afraid of each other. You were the same. You really resembled each other. Truly mother and daughter."

Then I went off in the company of my footsteps through the immense silence of the field of graves. Perhaps I had no thoughts as I walked peacefully; long moments without haste, without words to be prepared for others or for myself. Dark winter afternoons, blond spring evenings. I passed beneath the great portal, I went off along the wall, in front of San Lorenzo, I crossed the street, I stepped onto the long sidewalk opposite, near the institute. I knew that farther ahead Diego was waiting for me. I felt, gradually, as I walked, his presence come nearer. I walked with my eyes down, still clasping my solitude tightly while, from the void, painfully, thoughts took shape, then words, which I had to prepare for him. I would have postponed to infinity that meeting which I knew I wanted, but my legs moved fast.

Then there was one spring evening when I was wearing a pair of little low brown shoes, with a strap. The end of the strap was cut in a triangle, I remember, and was curled up. The tap of my steps went from heels to the wall, echoed, and I followed that game of duplication.

"Hello, darling."

He had moved from the wall beside me while I thought he was still far off, and perhaps I wasn't thinking of him yet. It was a jolt. At that moment I saw—or thought of—the innocent pink and white campanulas which had grown among the tram tracks nearby, in the sun, in the silence, and suddenly in the noisy shadow when the tram arrived. We had already greeted each other and were walking together, but that moment lasted and I was upset, offended as never before that my solitude had been shattered. The campanulas between the tram tracks. He talked. We were already farther on and he was talking. I walked at his side, I looked at the wrinkles at the corners of his eyes, his little nose, his mobile lips I knew I loved. I went on looking at those irrepressible lips and I felt an old sensation of the abyss, a mad desire to flee: as I had felt, a child, before the mirror. I drew back with horror and looked again at my shoes, which were walking along the sidewalk, one, the other, one, the other, trying to stun myself with my steps: in vain. And suddenly it was clear: the deceit with which I had tried to nourish myself, to pretend my solitude wasn't real and that Diego existed for me. Instead, he didn't exist: he was some hair, wrinkles around the eyes and lips that were never still; he, like all the others, like everything around me.

"Hey, Marzia, are you asleep? I was saying, Is this institute of yours really so important? I mean, is it true that you have a Nobel winner in there? What do you give him to eat, nectar and ambrosia? Tell me something about him. Do you know him?"

"The Nobel winner . . . yes, of course, I've seen him a few times, in the corridor, that's all. . . ."

"You've seen him in the corridor. You talk like a little girl. You have to toe the line in there, eh? I bet you walk slowly and stick close to the wall in the corridor, no?"

Close to the wall. Yes, it was true. And now he was making me see it. Like Lucia: only like Lucia. I looked at his free hand, which moved in the air; I thought I was playing an old game and I surely wasn't the first to do it: the campanulas were rhetoric, meanness. Desperately I sought a bit of gentleness in myself; I could still, I could still . . .

But they didn't come. The words overlapped, piled up, thick, invincible. Then the void. I heard in that void that the tram was approaching rapidly with its idiotic clanging bell.

I stopped. The tram reached the top of the street; before the descent, it clanged again, then charged down toward the cemetery, changing its sound. I had started running up the hill.

"Where are you going? Wait!" Diego said, overtaking me and grasping my arm. I freed myself, ran on, crossed the street just in time to jump into a bus. He remained behind. I smiled at him while the bus drove away. I was lying, with that smile; I waved to him again, at length, my face serious once more after he—I calculated—couldn't see me. I watched him grow small, wave at me again; then no more.

AT HOME I MADE myself some broth. I watched it while it simmered, I ate it without appetite. I went to write, and this time it would be a real letter. "Now," I began, "you will think this is the first time I've written you, and you will surely be a bit surprised, perhaps very surprised. I try to imagine how and when you will open this letter, but I can't, I don't even know how I will send it to you."

I told him then that I had left him like that because I didn't want to see him again; I had always deceived him; all my life I had pursued only words, desiring only them, idolizing them; and I had hated other people because I couldn't talk, I had loved them because I couldn't talk; because of my stammer—I used the word, finally—I had left my mother alone. I said that when he talked to me I didn't listen to him; I preferred to listen only to myself, the thousand words I would have liked to say. And our walks had been silences full of words addressed to him. Each evening, I confessed, I had written him; I had a drawer full of letters for him,

109

Diego. . . . "I was with you, you talked to me, you looked into my eyes and I was thinking: I'll write to him this evening. . . ."

I took an envelope from the study, sealed the letter and went to sleep.

The next day was Saturday and I had a free afternoon, but I telephoned Diego and said I was working on something and I would have to go to the institute and stay there until late. He wasn't to wait for me. He said he would use those hours to deal with various matters.

And so I would make the visit I had in mind before carrying out my other plan. Since my mother's death I hadn't seen Elena and I wanted to see her again; I wanted to see her house, Diego's. As I went away, I would leave the letter for him with his mother. The rest would come later.

The house was in Via dei Serpenti, on the left, going down the hill.

The vestibule was as narrow as the door onto the street, but not dark; in the back, a glass wall was filled with light. At one side the stairway began, tall steps made of stone. I had come to look: I proceeded slowly. To see the house, to see Elena again. I wanted this with an intensity to which I abandoned myself, in those moments, without questions.

I started climbing. The old stairway, with columns supporting the flights, had broad openings, unprotected by panes or shutters; as if suspended, it looked out over an immense court composed of terraces at various levels. I measured, stretched out before me, like a piece of music, the time it would take to arrive at the top floor, where I was not expected. This was the last time all for me, alone, and so I savored it.

I climbed up slowly. I looked and felt around the wooden railing, burnished and shined by hundreds of hands; the

110

stained, peeling walls; the dark-painted doors; real or imagined odors beyond the closed doors. Diego has always had these stains in his eyes, I said; every time he leaves or comes home he looks at them. And I tried to see in the peelings and stains the shapes that his imagination as a child had seen and perhaps still saw. At each landing I looked out over the great spaces of the courtyards and terraces, with plants and cats, skylights and railings, which at each floor shifted distances and perspectives.

I climbed up; rooftops appeared and chimney pots, while cats and terraces became smaller. And suddenly—but not at once, not the first time I looked—I saw the big lizard on the wall opposite. The first was a surprising, enormous relief of a gecko, and farther on there was a crocodile, which was no bigger than the gecko. Then a huge lizard. They must have been plaster. They had no architectonic function; they were on the wall opposite, among the windows, white and gray, bigger than a window. I stopped.

And he never told me! He's always lived here, he sees them every day; he never said a word about them! Maybe the street is named after them, I thought; but it wasn't important. I climbed lightly, now, with eyes and thoughts only for the huge lizards made of wall. Diego never told me! I reached the last flight, running, laughing; because he, who talked so much, he who said everything, always, without blocks and without effort, had never told me about the lizards. And I was still laughing when I pressed the little button of yellowed bone in the last door. The bell was just inside. I sensed faintly the odor that I knew as Elena's, which now seemed to emanate from the dark paint of the door. That odor brought me back, urgently, to memories, to the self I didn't love; and in the grip of apprehension, I already regretted ringing and I was ready to flee. And yet, inside, nothing happened and I waited a little; then I rang again, and it was as if I had had that yellow button beneath my finger every day of my life. The bell sounded nearby, then deep silence. I listened carefully, now. I peered into that silence, as the odor of the house breathed through the crack between the two wings of the door. Shyly, inside, a canary tested the air with a few trills. There, that was what the silence a moment before had been: the canary had stopped singing at the sound of the bell. It sang full volume now. It must be near a window, perhaps the cage was hung on the handle, because the glass panes seemed to echo that steely trill. On the right, yes, the window with the canary was on the right, there, a few feet into the room that I couldn't see, one of the few rooms, perhaps only two, of the house, and the window opened onto the same huge courtyard and the roofs, roofs and walls of houses now deep red in the last sun, which cast a sanguine reflection against a distant glass.

I rang again, but in fun, to make the bird stop again and to hear him resume his singing. I knew now that only he was in the house and Elena wasn't there. "It was Elena who kept canaries, but you can't remember; I took you there, but you were still a tiny baby." Elide, her soft fluent voice, which had died before she did. Only Elena remembered that voice.

I moved from the door, I looked out again and I thought that in an instant I could have flown over the great spaces of the courtyards. I stayed like that a long time; then slowly I went down a floor, two floors, and looked out again. The lizards were there, in centuries' ambush on the wall opposite, in relief and unreal in the blue and violet near-darkness of the summer evening, among windows which were coming alight and which were ignorant of them. I had kept so many things from Diego, and I had written him other things, but he didn't know about them. He had never told me about the

112

lizards. I imagined telling him that. He would have looked at me with gentle eyes and said, "What? Didn't I tell you that on the wall opposite my house there are those beasts?" And then, "Hmph, it's true I never told you. Well, don't let it bother you!"

It was as if I heard him. I laughed. I laughed a long time to myself, my throat caught in a happy knot as the illuminated windows danced in my clouded eyes and, above, the dark blue sky. Footsteps were coming up, a door was opened above me, then slammed. "Don't let it bother you!" I heard in my ears, in my throat. I opened my purse, took out the letter sealed in the envelope and tore it across, then again, into tiny pieces that I dropped and then watched flying in the almost black air of the courtyard. I waited until they had all settled on the terraces and plants, engulfed by the darkness. I ran down the rest of the steps, almost dancing; I found myself in the street.

At home I took those papers from the drawer, I folded them, sheet by sheet, and made a little packet. Then I went into my mother's room and took a thriller from the shelf. In bed I read half of it. "The rest tomorrow," I said aloud, putting down the book and turning off the light.

IT WAS SUNDAY. A sphere of sun came into my mother's room, as it had so many other times in those years. I sat on the bed that I should have dismantled and given away. The memory of the previous evening could hardly bear the immodest light of the day, the shapeless Sunday time, while I looked at the shaft of light that moved with the ancient, dancing dust. Then the phone rang. Diego, I thought. I didn't move, prey to myself, as of old. I stayed and listened to the almost tangible bell of the black machine, the round smile of its numbers, beyond, on the desk in the study. I looked at the stripe of sunlight, I listened to the immobility of my legs, I measured the sounds and the intervals between sounds. White moments, black moments—silences and sound—great spaces I ran across, like an ant in an animated cartoon. I didn't want to talk to him, not even on the phone. Finally it did not ring again. I looked up to the mirror where, as a child, I had made faces to frighten myself. Immobile, I stared at those eyes. Then, dizzy, I lowered mine.

The woman came to clean, and I fled that room.

Diego would call me again, he would come. I had to warn him off, not let him find me. I dressed hastily but carefully, combing my hair neatly and putting on make-up. I took the packet of written pages and went out. At the door downstairs I turned quickly to the right, my back to the street along the river, as if he were already appearing there.

I went down Via Muzio Clementi, Via Pietro Cossa, walking briskly, enjoying the perspective flight of the buildings and the stones on the ground. I heard the water from the drinking fountain, louder than the other days, because it was Sunday. A cat was lying on the sidewalk. I turned the corner toward Piazza Cavour, in front of the Waldensian church, and I looked back into Via Marianna Dionigi. I saw him at once. He was there, on the deserted pavement in front of the building, his newspaper open. He looked up at the windows, then at his wristwatch. I saw him fold the paper again, run his parted fingers through his hair in the old gesture full of echoes, cross the street, go inside. I calculated the time he would take to go up, the woman at the door telling him I had gone out, his coming down again.

He reappeared. He turned firmly toward the Tiber without looking around. I followed him rapidly, reaching the river when he was almost at the bridge. Now he was walking slowly. The bridge was empty, bright, with eddies of Sunday dust. I had almost overtaken him, I was following him now at a few paces, and I observed him. He walked bent over, flinging his feet out carelessly. I saw how ugly his shoes were with the heels worn toward the outside. His right foot moved more awkwardly than the other, making a little turn in the air before striking the ground. I had in me, in a knot, all the questions I didn't ask myself. I looked at the river's water between the little columns that ran beside my steps. I was holding the packet of letters tight.

The traffic light changed pointlessly, there was no one there. Diego crossed on the red light. I waited for it to turn green.

He had gained ground with the traffic light. I saw him walk on, bent, his hands in his pockets, swaying, the folded newspaper tight under his elbow, toward the low wall that surrounds the little garden. Perhaps a foot between the wall with its movie posters and his arm. I heard how my footsteps would be, hard on the sloping sidewalk, if I started running.

Fontanella Borghese. Opposite, at the end, Trinità dei Monti.

I continued following him. I looked at the ugly, runover shoes I loved, the defenseless nape; beyond his head, the steps and the church in the sun. Too bad there were all those wires and those black knots against the sky. It would have been beautiful to see the church and the sky without those wires. I narrowed my eyes, trying to erase the wires. "Don't let it bother you. . . ."

Suddenly I succeeded. I no longer saw the wires, or the black knots.

About the Author

ALESSANDRA LAVAGNINO was born in Naples, Italy, and has lived in Rome and in Palermo, where she currently lives with her husband and their three children. Educated in Rome, she took a degree with honors in biology at the University of Rome, writing a thesis on insecticide-resistant flies. She has also obtained a post-graduate diploma in animal biology. *The Lizards* is her first novel, and in 1968 it received a national award for a first novel by an unpublished writer.